ASHER

A Demons-In-Law Novel

LOUISA MASTERS

Asher

Copyright © 2023 by Louisa Masters

Cover: Booksmith Design

Editor: Hot Tree Editing

ASHER

When your imaginary boyfriend turns up in your hometown, marriage is the only option.

I'm not anti-relationship, but my life is good right now, and love is not a priority. Too bad my grandmother disagrees. People say she's scary, and sure, some of her enemies went missing under mysterious circumstances, but she loves me and wants the best for me… which, right now, is marriage. The matchmaking is a lot, and she's not letting up. What's a demon to do except invent a long-distance boyfriend?

That backfires hard when the one-night stand I based my fake boyfriend on arrives in our tiny village. Garrett's here to help our cut-off town assimilate with the rest of the Community of Species. He's not expecting to find he has a boyfriend he knew nothing about.

It doesn't take me long to convince him to agree to my new plan. I need the matchmaking to stop; he needs our insular little community to accept and trust him. The perfect solution: marriage. A business agreement with a time limit.

Just business.

Until he demands more. A sexy, nerdy hellhound in my bed isn't a deal breaker.

But as we get closer to our end date, it gets harder for me to imagine life without him. And when my little cousin goes missing, it's Garrett who saves the day… and reveals secrets the village didn't know we had.

CHAPTER ONE

Garrett

THE INCESSANT RING of the phone drags me from deep sleep… and a rather nice sex dream involving an insatiable incubus and a desk. Whoever this is, I may just have to kill them.

"What?" I mumble, trying to make my mouth wake up.

"Hello, cuz!"

I blink into the dark room. What the actual bleeding fuck?

"Who is this, and why do you want me to get arrested for murder?"

"Aw, you don't recognize me? Your favorite cousin? That's not very nice." The annoyingly chipper voice has taken on a fake hurt tone, and my brain comes online enough to match it with a name. "I'm hurt. My heart is bleeding. I might need actual medical attention to get me through the pain of—"

"What do you want, Alistair? It's…" I pull the phone away from my face and squint at the display. "It's one thirty in the morning. I was sleeping."

"Oops," my cousin announces cheerfully. "I forgot about the time difference."

I'm not completely sure I believe him. For all his affable, fun-loving ways, Alistair is also a highly trained investigator and deadly military operative. His current job is on the crack team that works directly for the lucifer, the leader of all community species. The energetic, annoying, lovable kid I used to babysit might very well have forgotten that time zones exist, but the adult? He probably remembered but decided he wanted to speak with me anyway.

"What do you want?" I repeat. With Alistair, it's best to keep the conversation on track. The track you choose, that is. If he picks the track, fuck knows where you'll end up.

"No chance of a chat, then?" he asks in an injured tone. "It's been a while since we caught up. All sorts of things have happened in my life, and I'm sure yours too."

I sigh. "If I promise to call you in about eight hours for a long chat, will you let me go back to sleep?"

He gasps. "Eight hours? Do you have any idea what time it will be then? You'll wake me up before my alarm!"

I let silence convey my feelings.

"Oh, fine," he grumbles. "No chat. I do have a reason for calling, and it's important—and you'll thank me for it."

"I'm sure." I roll onto my side, balance my phone on the side of my face and ear, and close my eyes.

"No, really. Sam asked if I knew anyone who could help, and I instantly thought of you."

My eyes open. Sam? Does he mean the lucifer?

I wait.

"He's been asked by the demon species leader to assist with finding some teachers for their settlement in the Swiss Alps," he continues, and I relax, slightly disappointed. Hiring teachers? That's nothing special. Any community of species agency in Europe can manage that. "The town is cut off by snow for at least four months of the year, so they've had difficulty retaining anyone."

"I'll send you the contact details of some reputable agencies," I murmur. "Tomorrow." I've trained as a teacher several times in the two hundred and twenty or so years since I reached adulthood and am actually qualified to train teachers myself. I've worked in education quite a lot over the same span of time. It's a field that enables a great deal of observation for my true passion: social anthropology. It's also steadier money than anthropology, and there've been plenty of times I was glad for the backup career.

"No, I don't need agencies," he huffs. "I need *you*. Wake up and listen to me. This town has *only demons*. The smallest children don't even know that other species exist. Sam's been there the past few days, and one child thought he was broken because he didn't have horns like demons do."

My body and brain surge to full wakefulness, and I sit up, clutching the phone to my ear. "I'm sorry, what did you say? The children aren't aware of the existence of other community species?" That's huge. Immense. Mind-boggling.

"Not until they begin school and are taught about them. From books. Because there are no other species there for them to interact with." Alistair sounds smug now. He knows he has my attention, damn him.

I toss back the covers and get up, walking through the dark house toward my study so I can turn on the computer. My mind is racing in a thousand directions.

"And they need teachers?"

"Yes. They have *none* right now, Garrett. None. Unwilling, untrained parents are being forced to homeschool with no real oversight or guidance."

I shudder as I flip on the desk lamp beside my computer. There are some excellent homeschooling programs out there, and some parents that excel at it, but not when they're unwilling, unguided, and lacking any kind of structured program.

"What is it they've asked for?" I open a new document to take notes and switch my phone to speaker so my hands are free.

"I emailed you their school's job criteria thingy," he says. "But in addition to that, any applicant needs to speak English, Italian, and one other language fluently, and can't have been associated with any cults or anti-government groups."

I snort as I skim through my emails, looking for his. "As if I'd allow children to be exposed to that kind of rhetoric." I spent twenty or so years once researching the nature of cults and how they affect the psyche of children, and it convinced me irrevocably of how dangerous they are, whether on a small, extremist scale or a larger, more mainstream one.

Scanning the job spec, I find it pretty standard—except that they require a minimum of ten years teaching experience. "Tell me about the school," I prompt. I've already assumed it's small, since the village is isolated and there are no teachers left at all.

"Uhhh… I think Sam said there's about seventy-ish kids. And they need two teachers—one for the little ones, and one for the older kids. I guess there's probably a building with classrooms too?"

I roll my eyes, considering. If there are only two teachers for all the children, it makes a little more sense that they want experience. There would be no staff backup, no group to talk over issues with. "Who acts as principal?" I ask. "One of the teachers, or someone else?"

"Garrett, cuz, I have no clue. I can put you in touch with the people who know. Can I tell Sam you'll help us find people?"

Excitement stirs slowly in my gut as I Google Maps the location of the settlement. Alistair wasn't wrong when he said the Swiss Alps. This place is smack bang in the middle, and not close to anywhere else. "You can tell him I'll help. But I don't think we'll need to find people."

There's a confused pause. "Do you have some locked in your basement or something? Because I gotta tell you, Sam frowns on that kind of thing."

Sometimes I wonder if my aunt dropped him on his head when he was a baby. And then stepped on him a few times. "No, Alistair. I don't have anyone locked in my basement."

"Then why won't we need to find anyone?"

I stare at the location pinned on the map. "Because I'll do it myself."

♏

THREE WEEKS LATER, I let the door of my hotel room close behind me, then wait five cautious seconds to make sure nobody's going to knock before letting out a sigh of relief and dropping my overnight bag. I'm a little more cautious with my laptop bag, because this is my fifth laptop of the year already, and it's not quite September yet. I keep forgetting technology isn't as sturdy as people.

Stepping over both, I close the distance to the bed and fall onto it. The mattress is amazing. I must remember to thank the demons who're paying for this incredible five-star hotel. Hopefully their willingness to put me up in luxury now will equate to a willingness to listen to my advice later, when I'm living in their isolated village in the alps, trying to educate their children and turn their town into a haven for all species. Because Alistair left a few things out during our conversation, like the fact that Lucifer Sam and the village council have decided they need to attract other species to live there. As far as I can tell, the main problem seems to be how cut off the town is during winter. It's not a problem for demons, who can teleport, but other species find the isolation difficult.

As a social anthropologist, this kind of situation is heaven. The village council have asked me to assess whether there might be any other hurdles to making Hortplatz attractive for non-demons, and I get to observe how demons function in isolation. Maybe I'll even get to see some of their more private ceremonies. Demons are fanatically protective of their important rituals, and not many outsiders get to witness them, even when the demons are fully integrated with other species. I'll step carefully, though. I've found it's always wise to be cautious when dealing with smaller, more isolated groups. Although a village of a thousand people isn't *that* small, comparatively.

Regardless of whether they welcome me with open arms or stonewall me at every turn, I'm excited about this opportunity. Social anthropology is my passion and my current career. Studying people and figuring out why and how they make up groups and societies is the most fascinating thing in existence, and anyone who says otherwise is clearly wrong. A group of children who've never known any species other than their own? Fascinating.

I'm only slightly annoyed that I now owe Alistair a favor for sending this my way. I love my cousin—really, I do—and sometimes I even like him, but he's so damn annoying. And now he's all smug because he's pulled this off. He was unbearable when he introduced me to the lucifer—his best friend, Sam.

Lucifer Sam was thrilled to have me take on the job, since it saved him having to interview people. I'm still not entirely sure how he even came to be involved—he doesn't live in the village, or even on the same continent, doesn't have a child in the school, and isn't even a demon. When I politely asked, he just shuddered, shook his head, and muttered, "Damaris." Alistair grinned and told me all would be made clear eventually.

The agreement we settled on, with Lucifer Sam and his demon boyfriend, Gideon (terrifying man, seriously), acting as representatives for the village, was that I'd oversee the classes and curriculum, basically acting as principal in conjunction with the village council, while the two post-doc researchers—both qualified teachers themselves—I've brought with me will do most of the hands-on teaching. This will allow us to also do the groundwork for the paper I plan to publish. The village council expressed some concern initially about my research, but I assured them of anonymity, and the lucifer showed them my research credentials, and that satisfied them. I'll be there for the entire school year, during which time I'll put together a comprehensive plan for ways they can attract other species to their village.

Then I'll send my team home and spend the summer helping them recruit new teachers while I write my paper. My leave of absence from Cambridge is only for twelve months, but by then, there should be at least a few new people of other species living in the village, which might help to overcome the other negatives—that it snows for most of the year and for at least four months, they'll be dependent on demons teleporting them places if they want to leave. I'm not a fan of being teleported by demons—the post-teleport sickness hits me hard. It's part of the reason I insisted on driving from England. Sure, I'd like to have my car with me this year, but also, the thought of a long-distance teleport almost convinced me not to go.

Too bad Annie, one of my researchers, gets car sick. We broke the drive down over three days to make it easier for her, but she's still had a tough time. I don't know why she didn't take me up on the offer to fly instead. But her misery has led Sid, my other researcher who has a poorly hidden crush on her, to fall completely apart. I've basically been babysitting them both for the past day and a half.

I wriggle to settle more comfortably on the bed. That's all over for now. I've got two nights in this delightful hotel in Zurich to relax before we drive south into the alps. Jesse, the demon species leader who's in charge of the village, suggested this break. Apparently the road into town is difficult.

So… since I'll be working responsibly in a small village for the next year, I plan to have a little nap now, maybe a room service dinner, and then go out and find someone to fuck me into oblivion for twenty-four hours. Then I'll kick him out, get a good night's sleep, and be ready to tackle my new project.

It's the perfect plan.

CHAPTER TWO

Asher

I'M EXCELLENT AT MATH. Honestly, it's a gift. Some people can paint, others can understand complicated legal issues. I look at a page of complex equations and just *know* what the answer is… and why.

But the kind of math I'm trying to do right now… not so much. Because seriously, the biggest variable in this equation is how mad my grandmother would be if I ignored her call, and nobody can predict something like that. The woman changes emotional direction faster than a windsock in a tornado.

Sighing, I answer. "Hi, Grandmother."

"Hello, Asher. Were you busy?"

See? A subtle rebuke over how long it took me to pick up. Now I either have to lie to her or admit I didn't want to answer… and she can sense a lie from halfway around the world, my cousin Gideon assures me.

"I was trying to work out an equation," I prevaricate. It's not totally a lie.

"I see." The disapproving edge to her voice is a clear indication that she sees right through me. "I won't keep you too long, then. I wouldn't want family to interfere with your busy and important life."

Just kill me now.

"Nothing's more important than family," I assure her, and sincerity rings in my tone. I believe that wholeheartedly. It's just that Grandmother's idea of family priorities is vastly different from mine.

"True," she agrees. "Are you seeing anyone?"

There it is. Her current priority: marrying me off so I'll get started on producing the next generation. Part of me understands why she's in a hurry. As a species, our fertility rate is super low. It can take decades or centuries to conceive, and she's probably only got three or four hundred years left. Maybe five, at a stretch. If she's going to hold her great-grandchildren, someone has to get started making them.

On the flip side, I don't want that someone to be me. I like being single, and I'm not ready to think about kids, even if I was seeing someone.

"Not right now, Grandmother." I cringe and wait for the reply I know is coming.

"Excellent! I was talking to a friend this morning, and she mentioned her daughter will be in Zurich this weekend. It would be so kind if you could take her to dinner, maybe show her around the city."

Well, at least this isn't as bad as when she invited three people to dinner and told me to take my pick.

"That sounds like it would be fun, but I can't." I manage to make myself sound regretful. "I'm coming back home on Friday, and I'll be based there for a few weeks, at least." I enjoy spending time in Zurich and managing the family's business interests, but nothing is better than home with my family. We've only lived in Switzerland for the past half century or so, but I love it.

"Oh. You'll be home? Well, I suppose she'll have to find her way around on her own. I've missed you." I can hear the smile in her voice, and my annoyance at her matchmaking fades. She loves us—I've never doubted that.

"Maybe I can meet up with her another time," I find myself saying, like an idiot.

"We can sort that out later. I'm glad you'll be back. The new teachers are coming this week, and I'm not sure if I was right to agree to all this. Jesse's asked me to host the welcome dinner. You'll come, of course—I'd appreciate your opinion of them."

I roll my eyes. "Of course." Like she needs anyone's opinion except her own. The woman's sharper than a tack. I *am* interested to meet these new teachers, though. My seven-year-old sister is still in school, and it's been a pain in the ass trading off homeschooling duties with my parents this past year. Half the time I have no clue what I'm supposed to be teaching her. Or she'll ask a question I can't answer, like "what kind of tree is the tallest and do birds nest at the top?" Google has become my best friend.

It's a little concerning that they're not just teachers. Anthropologists, Gideon said, who want to write a research report on a single-species town and how that's affected us and the children. They *are* teachers, though, with plenty of experience, and most important, they're not demons. A hellhound, a sorcerer, and a succubus, Gideon told me. That should give the children a decent orientation to other species until we can start attracting them to live in the village.

Grandmother asks me to bring her a few things from her favorite shops—yay for me—then ends the call with the imperious order to let her know what time I'll be arriving.

I drop my phone onto my desk and stare blankly at the

computer screen, thoughts of teachers, matchmaking, and old lady shopping whirling through my head. Two out of three aren't really issues, but I've got to find a solution to the matchmaking. How do I convince Grandmother to let it go?

A conversation I had with my cousins when Gideon and his boyfriend—who happens to be the lucifer, the leader of the community of species—visited a month ago pops into my head. It's ridiculous, but could the solution be to find a sensible, like-minded person willing to marry me in a business deal just to get Grandmother off my back? We could have contracts and out clauses and agree to dissolve the whole thing if we meet people we want to marry for real.

I snort. I can't seriously be considering this. No, there's another solution; I just haven't thought of it yet. What I need is a few hours away from my desk to clear my head.

Glancing at the time, I see business hours are well and truly over. No wonder my stomach's growling. I'll head down to the pub and see about a meal and a drink… and maybe some company for the night, to clear the cobwebs away.

𝔐

"Is this seat taken?"

I look up from my drink at the man standing opposite, his hand resting lightly on the back of the booth. A beer bottle dangles loosely from his other hand, and there's a small, suggestive smile on his attractive face.

"Be my guest."

He slides into the booth as I push aside my empty dinner plate and covertly study him. He's a shifter—hellhound would be my guess, based on his six-foot-plus stature—with curly mid-brown hair and brown eyes in an attractive face. It's a whole checklist of ticks for me… as long as he's okay with casual.

"I'm Asher," I offer, and his smile widens.

"Garrett. I'm only here for a couple of days and want some company."

His bluntness only increases my attraction to him, and I smile back, making sure to over-emphasize it. Demon facial expressions are a lot more subtle than other species', and that's led to them thinking we never smile and are always grouchy. "That's great, because I'd love a couple of days of low-key company."

He takes a sip from his drink and asks, "Work in finance?"

I snort. "How'd you guess?"

"You have the 'I spend all day squinting at numbers' line between your eyes. Plus, this is Zurich. It was a safe guess."

Laughing, I salute him with my glass. "Are you saying I have wrinkles?" I know exactly which line he's talking about, dammit.

Garrett shrugs. "I'm not interested in kids who don't know how to find a prostate. Age means experience. Is that an issue for you?"

I shake my head. "It's stupid how much we have in common."

This time, it's his turn to laugh. "The desire for sex with someone who knows how to get you off is only one thing."

"I like that brand of beer, too," I counter, gesturing at the bottle. "And we both have conservative haircuts." I glance around and lower my voice, even though none of the humans around us are paying attention. "Both members of the community. Both want fun with no strings."

"We're practically the same person," he deadpans.

We talk for a little longer about nothing in particular, and then I feel a foot nudge my ankle. There's no shoe on it, and it slowly slides up my calf. I can take a hint, so I knock back the rest of my drink. "Time to go?"

"Excellent idea. My hotel's only a block away." He slides out of the booth, and I follow suit.

"Let me pay my bill, and I'll meet you at the door."

Not quite ten minutes later, I follow him into a very nice hotel room. "Fancy," I comment as the door closes behind us. The golden glow of the lamps makes it all seem homey.

"Yeah," Garrett says, kicking off his shoes and heading toward the bed. "There are worse places to spend a night." He pulls his shirt off and tosses it aside. "Are you just going to stand there all night?"

I don't need to be invited twice. I unbutton my collar and yank my shirt off over my head, then start working on my pants as I move to join him. "Anything I should know?" Wow, he's lovely naked. His skin is the kind of pale that only spending most of your life indoors will achieve, and while he has the tall, broad frame typical of a hellhound, he's not gym buff. I love the hints of softness.

"I want to be fucked, and I like to be petted."

"I like an uncomplicated man. Lube?"

"Dammit." He gets off the bed and heads for the bathroom, and I take advantage of the chance to get the rest of my clothes off. When he comes back, lube in hand, I pat the mattress beside me.

"Kissing okay?" he asks as he climbs back onto the bed. I reply by leaning over to press my lips to his. They're soft, slightly chapped, and open eagerly to me. Within seconds, I'm rolling him under me, grateful he's almost as big as me and I don't need to worry about crushing him. Sex is so much better when I can manhandle my partner and not damage him.

From the growl that escapes him as he wraps his legs around my thighs, he's on board. The action causes me to settle between his legs, my hard-as-stone cock rubbing against his, and I flex my hips, trying to get another growl out of him. He obliges, then breaks the kiss. "Go fast and take the edge off. We can take our time for round two."

Not gonna argue with that. I pull away and look for the lube, finding it abandoned on the mattress beside us. "Ride me," I order, propping myself against the pillows as I flip open the cap.

"Give me that." He reaches for the travel-sized bottle.

"I can—"

"Yeah, but I'll be faster. Just lie there and enjoy the show."

It's like I dreamed of the perfect man and then he showed up and wanted to have sex with me. I obey orders and relax into the pillow, eyes locked on his fingers as he squats on the mattress and preps himself. At one point, his breath catches and I drag my gaze up his body to his face, taking in the edge-of-pain pleasure there.

"Okay?" I murmur, getting up on my knees and moving close enough to run my hands down his upper arms.

He nods, opening his eyes. "I love this part. Kiss me."

Careful not to disturb his balance, I take his mouth, capturing his little growl and every gasp as he continues to stretch himself. Remembering what he said about being petted, I lightly stroke his shoulders and—

"Ooomph!" I land on my back on the mattress. "What—"

"Let's go." He knee-walks to me and straddles my hips. "It's been a long time since I've been with a demon. I forgot how thick you all are." His big hand wraps around my cock, and my breath stutters in my chest.

"Sure you can take me?" I taunt, and he chuckles.

"I can't wait." He drizzles lube over my dick, then drops the bottle on my stomach. I grab it and lube up my hand. His hard, long cock is pointing toward me, and I have plans for it.

I wait for Garrett to position himself and ease down. My cockhead presses against his pucker, and it takes a moment and some pressure for him to relax enough to let me in. He slides slowly down, giving himself time to adjust, and it's not until I'm all the way in and he's grinning wickedly at me that I grab his dick. "Set the rhythm, hellhound."

He rises off me. "Keep up, demon."

When he said he wanted this first time to be fast, he wasn't lying. And for someone who doesn't have a gym-honed body, he's got amazing strength in his thighs. The pace he sets is fast and hard, and it's not long before I'm soaked in sweat, clenching my teeth to keep from exploding inside his hot, tight ass. My hand is pumping his cock, and he's gasping on every stroke, his face flushed, eyes glassy.

I'm on the verge of rolling him under me so I can take control and finish us both when I feel them. Against my palm, the soft-rigid touch of cartilage.

His barbs.

Barbs only pop out when a shifter is about to come.

With one last squeeze, I give myself over to my orgasm, letting it blast through me even as Garrett throws back his head with a yell. A moment later, he collapses onto my chest, right in the warm mess he just sprayed over me. He's heavy, and I roll us onto our sides so we can catch our breath.

"That was fucking incredible," I gasp, running my hand over his torso and tilting my head to lay a kiss on his neck.

"Five minutes, and we go again."

This might just be the best night of my life.

CHAPTER THREE

Garrett

"They weren't kidding when they said the road was bad," Annie observes from the passenger seat beside me. She's pale with a greenish tinge and looks clammy, but so far has managed not to be sick today. The new travel sickness meds might be working… sort of. "If they want to keep people here who need to use the road regularly, they're going to need to improve it."

I hum in agreement. "That's definitely going into my plan," I mutter, trying to steer around the biggest pothole and managing to hit half a dozen others. If I didn't have my team and pile of bags in the car, I'd abandon it here, shift, and run the rest of the way. "We must be close, though." I hope. We're so far up in the mountains now that the air is much thinner, and it's definitely cooler. If this is what it's like in August, I can believe that they get cut off by snow for the whole of winter and then some.

Luckily, it's less than an hour later, even at the stupidly slow pace I'm forced to drive at, that the thinning trees open up to show a picture-perfect village that looks like it belongs in a movie.

"Ohhhhhh," Annie whispers.

"Wow, that's pretty," Sid adds. "I'm glad I brought my camera."

I don't say anything, just take in the lovely vista. With snowcapped peaks surrounding us, we're guaranteed an amazing view from every direction. That's a huge selling point.

Though maybe not so much in the winter when it's obscured by blizzards.

The car crawls along the main street of the village, past charming shops, a supermarket, what looks like a town hall, and a lovely green park where about a dozen children are playing. The five adults supervising them all turn to stare at my car, and I realize that there's no traffic. As in… literally none. The village is small, but not so small that I'd expect to see no cars at all, even on a clear day like this. This must be a demon thing—they incorporate teleportation into their lives the same way the rest of us use cars and public transport. Does that mean there are no cars in the village at all? There are roads, though. Did they build them for the aesthetic? Or are there some cars here?

"Sid, make a note about cars, please."

"Sure. Um… cars?"

"Yes. There aren't any."

He makes a wordless sound of surprise.

I turn right after the park, following the directions we were given, and find a small, neat building with a sign out front indicating it's the post office. I'm not sure how often they get mail delivery up here, given the state of the road we just drove in on, and I ask Sid to make another note as I park the car. Jesse, the demon species leader who acts as the mayor—though completely unelected—said his office and the town administration are based in this building.

Sid and I scramble out of the car and stretch, while

Annie drags herself out and leans against the low stone wall bordering the house next door. I tune into my sense of smell. Hellhounds have the best sense of smell of any species, so much so that most of us learn how to ignore it while we're still small children. It's too distracting otherwise, and can also kind of invade people's privacy, since we can smell changes in emotion. So while I can always smell those things, I don't actually process them unless I'm concentrating. The rest of the time it just gets shunted to another part of my brain, like background noise.

Now, though, I focus on my olfactory intake. There's nearly no pollution here, which is nice. The underlying scent is of demon, which makes sense, since they're the only ones who live here. I can pick out a few individual scents, people who've walked past here recently or are nearby. It's a little odd not having the mixed base smell of all species. I'm so used to smelling a combo of hellhound, felid, demon, sorcerer, incubus, vampire, and human. More recently, I've occasionally gotten a whiff of other that told me an elf or dragon had been around recently. But here, there's none of that. Just demon.

The front door of the post office opens, and a man comes out, his face sober in the way that demon faces always are. I've never spent too much time studying demons specifically—another reason this is such an exciting opportunity—but colleagues have told me that due to their denser muscle mass, demon facial expressions are less explicit than anyone else's. So a neutral face could mean nothing, or it could also mean they're happy to see us. The trick is to look for subtle relaxations and shifts.

"Dr. Smythe?" he calls, and I smile.

"Hello. Please call me Garrett. You must be Jesse, the species leader."

We meet halfway and shake hands. "It's so good to

meet you," he says, and I watch his face closely. "Thank you for co— Is there something on my face?" He lifts a hand to his mouth.

"No, I'm sorry." I shake my head. "I'm trying to learn to read demon facial cues. I didn't mean to make you uncomfortable." Note to self: their own subtle muscle movements allow them to read other species' expressions more easily. I'm not going to be able to hide what I'm feeling here.

"Oh!" His face barely changes, but because I'm paying such close attention, I get the impression of pleasure. "That's great. The children aren't used to being around other people, so they don't exaggerate their expressions like we've learned to. You'll get plenty of practice with them."

I shoot a glance at Sid, wondering if he's paying close enough attention to guess what I'm thinking. He pulls out his notebook to scribble something. I hope it's "educate newcomers on demon subtlety" and not "teach kids to make faces."

Waving them forward, I introduce Jesse to my team, and he greets them both with handshakes and thanks for being here. Demons have a reputation for being grumpy, but that's not strictly true. They do tend to have short tempers and are more serious-minded than hellhounds, for example—my species' reputation for levity is well-earned —but mostly they get a bad rap because of the whole rarely smiling thing. Jesse in particular seems to be quite laid-back.

"Are you going to keep them standing out there?" a new voice demands, and I look past Jesse to see an older woman in the doorway of the post office. The frown on her face makes me swallow hard. Other than that, though, she doesn't look angry at all—her hands are loosely by her sides, no foot tapping. Her posture is impeccable, and she's immaculately groomed. If I had to guess at her age, I'd say she's approaching her millennium.

"We're coming now," Jesse calls patiently. He turns back to me and lowers his voice a lot. "Some of the families here are very influential."

That's all he says, but I get the hint. This woman, whoever she is, is a member—possibly the matriarch—of one of those influential families. We hellhounds have them too, and while some are just pretentious pain-in-the-neck blowhards, others take their position and wealth seriously and do a lot for the community. I'm not sure what kind this woman belongs to, but based on Jesse's comment, it's not worth upsetting her.

We stroll to the building, and the woman steps aside to let us enter what looks like… a post office. It's unstaffed at the moment.

"Damaris, meet Dr. Garrett Smythe and his team, Dr. Annie Adarsh and Dr. Sid Lane. This is Damaris Bailey, who sits on the village council and is instrumental in the management of our settlement."

Bailey… a relative of Gideon, the lucifer's boyfriend? Gideon Bailey has been a high-ranking member of the lucifer's team for decades, beginning when the former lucifer, Percy Caraway, was in charge. Now that I think of it, his scowl is remarkably similar to Damaris Bailey's.

"It's a pleasure to meet you, ma'am." I don't offer my hand. I've been around long enough, and dealt with enough older members of the community, to know that she'd be offended if I did. The prerogative to shake hands is hers. "Thank you for allowing us to be here and compile our research."

She stares at me for a long moment with her piercing dark gaze. Sweat breaks out along my spine, and I force myself to remember that she's probably not planning to kill me and hide my body somewhere in the mountains. Behind me, I hear the familiar rustle of fabric that means Sid's squirming.

Finally, she holds out her hand. "Thank you for coming, Dr. Smythe. Your academic history is impressive. I'm sure you'll be adequate for this task."

Not sure if she's put me in my place or complimented me, I shake her hand and smile.

"The rest of the council is waiting," Jesse says diplomatically. "Let's go through."

Damaris turns away, freeing me from her gaze, and it takes everything in me not to sag and fan myself in relief. I really want to shift into my hellhound form and feel the reassurance of claws and teeth. Instead, I ask Jesse how often the mail is delivered up here.

"It's not," he informs me. "We have a post office box in Zurich where all our mail is delivered. Our postmaster teleports there daily to collect it, then will deliver what he can. The post office is open for two afternoons a week for people to collect anything else."

It's not the worst system I've ever heard of. But it would only work for demons. It also seems like a lot of work for one person—there are a thousand people living here, and even though letters are on the decline, online shopping is not. I make a mental note to interview the postmaster.

Jesse leads us through an archway into a wide hall. "Over here is the town management office. Any requests for permits or neighborly disputes are managed here. Our administrator is Bethany." He gestures through an open doorway at a woman sitting behind a desk, talking on the phone. She glances up, sees us, and waves. I *think* her face changed a little to show… interest?

This is going to be a steep learning curve.

"And here is the main meeting room."

We walk through a doorway into a... meeting room. There's a boardroom table surrounded by chairs, five of which are filled.

Damaris takes a seat near the head of the table, and Jesse introduces us to everyone before we find places to sit. "We won't keep you long," he promises. "I know the road is rough, and you must want to relax and refresh yourselves. We have a lovely five-bedroom house ready for you, and I'll take you there as soon as we're done. We've hired a housekeeper for you, and I know they want to discuss your requirements."

I glance over at Annie. She's got color back in her face and seems a lot better, so I nod. "Of course. We have some initial plans based on your existing curriculum, but we think it might be best to meet the students before we finalize anything. Children learn in different ways."

Damaris's expression changes somehow. Did her eyes narrow? What did I say that she disapproves of?

"Obviously your job only extends to the school-age children," another woman whose name I can't quite remember says. "But would it be possible to have the occasional session with the younger ones?"

"Yes. Of course." I don't hesitate. "My understanding is that they're not made aware of other species until they're school age?"

"It's not a rule," Jesse interjects. "We've looked into it, and some have been read stories with other species, or talked to older siblings. We haven't deliberately prevented them from knowing about the community." He sounds a little anxious, and I understand why. As a species leader, he'd be aware of the events several years back, where it was discovered that a cult was isolating species and indoctrinating them in an attempt to overthrow the government. It's not information that was widely shared, but with two cousins working directly for the lucifer, I sometimes hear things others don't. Elinor contacted me at the time to ask about the anthropological implications.

"I never thought you had," I assure them all, looking around the table and making eye contact with everyone. "We can set up a weekly playgroup of sorts, if you like? With the three of us representing three different species, that should enable them to get an idea that people can be different to them."

"What would it involve? We have babies and toddlers."

I look at Sid, whose doctorate was in early childhood development. This would be a good area for him to take the lead on.

"We'd let the children play—us just being in the room will be a new experience for them. Some won't immediately notice the differences in us, but they'll start getting used to our scent. There are some stories we can read that might begin a discussion, and if a few weeks pass without anyone asking any questions, Garrett could shift and show them his hellhound form." He slides me a sideways glance and sticks his tongue firmly in his cheek. "Few children can resist a puppy."

I refrain from smacking him, because it's true. And the few who do are usually afraid of dogs, which can be overcome by shifting back and showing them that I'm a familiar person. "The younger children will find it easier to accept us," I promise the council. "And of course we'd want parents or caregivers there as well."

That seems to satisfy them all, and their questions after that are more cursory. I think they didn't have a true agenda for this meeting, just wanted to meet us and get a feeling for our personalities.

Finally, Damaris says, "I think we can leave it there. School begins week after next, so you have a few days to settle in before you need to start lesson planning." She makes it sound like an order, and I bite my tongue to keep from telling her that our lesson planning has already begun. "I hope you'll all join me this weekend at a welcome party. Nothing too big, of course."

It's phrased like a request, but it's really not. She also doesn't sound happy about it, though I'm not sure if I'm just reading her wrong. "That sounds lovely." I manage not to add "ma'am," which is quite a feat given the tone of voice she used. It will be a good opportunity to meet some more people, anyway.

She stands, and that seems to be the cue for everyone to leave. I really need to find out—discreetly—more about her. Even if it means a call to Alistair.

Dammit.

CHAPTER FOUR

Asher

I STROLL out of the teleport room in the house I share with my cousins. As always, I spare a smug thought for the other species, schlepping places on foot or by car, plane, or other transit. Seconds ago I was in my apartment in Zurich, and here I am nearly a hundred and fifty kilometers from there. I'm fresh, relaxed, and ready to get on with my day.

The kitchen is my first stop, since I can smell coffee. It's been hours since I had a cup, and I need a hit before having dinner with Grandmother. I may have gotten out of her setup for this weekend, but that doesn't mean she's given up.

My cousin Micah looks up from his stool at the counter as I beeline for the coffee maker. "You're back," he says. Micah's always been one to state the obvious. "Grandmother said you were coming, but Zac and I figured you'd make an excuse at the last minute."

I pause with my coffee halfway to my mouth. "Why would I do that? This is my home."

He shrugs. "Yeah, but aren't you avoiding her while she's on her 'get Asher married' streak?"

Oh. Now I get it. "There's no avoiding it. She tried to set me up with the daughter of a friend who happened to be in Zurich this weekend. I figured I may as well come home and enjoy that, at least."

He makes a disinterested sound and goes back to the architecture magazine he's reading.

When the settlement moved fifty years ago and this village was built, Micah, Zac, and I decided to live together temporarily so there would be houses ready sooner for families. We thought about living with Grandmother, but that seemed a little too selfless… and stupid. This was a compromise we could live with. And we just haven't bothered to change things since. I'm in Zurich a lot of the time, and it's not like we don't all get along. We're the best of friends. The house is large, and we have a cleaner in once a week to keep us all in line. Until and unless one of us decides to marry and start a family, why bother to upset the status quo?

I slide onto a stool next to Micah and pull out my phone, settling in to enjoy twenty minutes of coffee and the financial blogs before I go to Grandmother's house for dinner with the family.

ᔕᗰ

"AsHER!" Chloe, my baby sister, hurls herself at me while I'm still in the doorway. "You're back!"

I pick her up, even though at seven she's started telling people she's too big for that now, and give her a squeezy hug. "I've only been gone two weeks," I tease. "And we Zoomed four times."

"I still missed you." She smacks a kiss on my cheek. "Nobody else reads with all the voices like you do."

Giving her a little jostle, I drill my forefinger into her

ribs, the resulting squeal of laughter making me smile. "Ah, so the truth comes out. It's not me you missed at all."

She squirms to be put down, and I obey. "Don't forget, story time later," she orders.

"Chloe," our father chides, "you can read to yourself now. Let Asher have the night off."

The look she gives him has entirely too much attitude in it. "Dad, this is between me and Asher. He can speak for himself."

Dad's eyebrow slowly rises, and I flash back to when I was on the receiving end of that eyebrow. It's an early warning alert… back down now, or that thing you want to do will be canceled. "Oh?"

Chloe's lips press together in a flat line, and she glares mutinously at him… then caves. Turning to me, she says, "If you have time later, a story would be nice. But it's okay if you don't." She makes sure to add a lip quiver and big, sad eyes.

Dad sighs and shakes his head, but he's fighting a smile.

"We'll see how the night goes," I tell her, knowing full well that I'll be reading at least one story. Probably more.

The smug little smirk comes back. "That means yes. Thanks, Asher!" She whirls and runs down the hall, shouting for our cousin Isaac, who at nearly five is closest to her in age.

I close the front door and look at Dad. "She's in a good mood."

He claps me on the shoulder and gives a little squeeze. "The new teachers arrived this week, and she's excited about going back to school."

"Me too," I say fervently. "I am so excited about her going back to school. And so, so glad I never thought about becoming a teacher myself."

Dad snorts as he leads me down the hall toward the living room at the back of Grandmother's house. "The whole world is glad you never thought about becoming a teacher."

Grandmother is waiting for us in the living room, and I bend to kiss her cheek. She's never been demonstrative, so I'd be shocked if she hugged me or anything like that.

"At last," she says, her tone implying I've kept her waiting for hours. "Where are your cousins?"

"Micah wanted to finish reading his magazine, and Zac's in the shower. They'll be here soon, but I didn't want to wait." I was hoping that would earn me points, but now I realize what a mistake it was to come without my cousins as a buffer. I need someone to make distracting comments when the matchmaking talk gets too intense, and definitely my other relatives won't. They're getting far too much enjoyment from this.

She sniffs, as though Zac showering is an insult to her —when, believe me, the insult would actually be if he didn't—and grabs my arm, towing me toward her favorite chair. She seats herself, then gestures for me to take the chair beside her.

Uh-oh. She wants to talk.

"I've been diversifying some of our investments lately," I start in a desperate attempt to sidetrack her, but she waves it off.

"Asher, I know you enjoy your carefree bachelor life, but we need to discuss your responsibilities."

Resentment pangs in my chest. I may be a bachelor, but I'm hardly carefree. I work sixty-plus hours most weeks, managing the vast array of our family's holdings and investments. Nobody else wanted to take it over when Grandfather died, so I'm the one who's maintained our fortune… and exponentially multiplied it. And I still make time to be here for the family and help with homeschooling and building this village. I even manage the settlement's funds. Doesn't that give me the right to enjoy my time off however I want to, even if that means a succession of no-strings affairs?

"Well," I begin, wondering how much of that I'll manage to say before Grandmother twists it around so I'm agreeing with her, but she doesn't even let me get the first point out.

"I was just like you when I was your age. Not quite your age… I met your grandfather when I was a little younger. But I didn't want to settle down either. I wanted to see the world and try new things and *explore*."

Does she mean…? Nausea takes me over at the thought of my grandmother *exploring*. Please let her mean she wanted to trek through a jungle or something.

"But marriage didn't mean I couldn't do all that. It just meant I had a partner to do it with me."

Fuck my life. I desperately try to suppress the thought of both my grandparents taking part in an orgy. She definitely means jungle trekking. Yep. Definitely.

"Grandmother, I know you only want the best for me. That you want me to have happy companionship and children of my own. But don't you agree that the most successful way for that to happen is for me to organically meet the right person and decide together how we want our future to be?" I give her my most persuasive look.

"No," she says bluntly. Across the room, my uncle chokes off a laugh. "Yes, I want you to meet the right person, but I've been waiting a hundred years for it to happen 'organically,' and it hasn't. So now we're going to do it mathematically. That should appeal to you."

I don't even know what to say to that. Where are Zac

and Micah? Why aren't they here to rescue me? "Mathematically?" I venture.

"Yes. Mathematically. You will make a list of qualities you're looking for in a partner. I'll take that list and use it to find potential spouses for you. Then I'll invite them here to meet with you, spend some time with you, and you can see if you click. Maybe I'll throw in some wild cards too," she muses. "Sometimes what we think we want isn't always right."

I blink at her, my mind racing to process this horrible idea. She's going to amplify the matchmaking scheme? Formalize it? And how is any of that mathematical?

"I'm sure once we expand the circle of interaction, you'll meet someone you can fall in love with in no time. We'll be planning a wedding within the year."

"I can't," I blurt. "I'm sorry, Grandmother, I can't."

Her gimlet stare zeroes in on me, and I swallow.

"What can't he do?" Zac asks cheerfully as he and Micah stroll in—too late to rescue me, dammit. How am I going to get out of this? If I didn't care so much about my grandmother and family, it would be easy—I'd say no and walk away. But it would break my heart to do that, and break their hearts… not to mention, she's doing all this because she genuinely wants the best for me. She's just… impatient and misguided. Apparently, my family needs to work on boundaries.

Grandmother narrows her eyes at my dad, who hurriedly explains the plan. Zac's eyes get wide. "Oh no, he can't do that."

"Why not?" The words are cold and sharp. Grandmother turns back to face me. "Why not, Asher? Don't you even want to try?"

Fuck. I open my mouth to admit defeat—

"He's seeing someone!"

My head whips around so fast, my neck cracks, and I gape at Micah. What is he *doing*?

"He's what?" Grandmother asks.

"He's seeing someone?" Dad echoes, exchanging a bewildered glance with my mother. "Did you know about this?"

She shrugs, her gaze on me. "He's all grown up now. He doesn't tell me his secrets anymore."

"Who are you seeing, Asher?" Chloe asks, she and Isaac watching me with interest. "Do you have a boyfriend or a girlfriend?"

This is a nightmare.

"Asher?" Grandmother prompts.

"I…" Fuck. What do I say? I don't want to lie to my family.

"He hasn't said anything because they've been taking it slow," Micah declares, clearly not sharing my aversion to lying to family. "His boyfriend isn't a demon, and he's not sure how he'd like living up here, but he doesn't want to cause friction with the family either."

Silence.

"Is this true, Asher?"

Mentally damning Micah while also grateful for the reprieve, I nod. It feels like less of a lie if I don't verbalize it.

She smiles. It's just a tiny one, small even for our species, but it's there. "Well, I like that he's taking such a respectful stance to your family. And of course I can understand his reservations about living here, given what we're going through at the moment. Perhaps he could visit for a weekend, though? See the village and form a proper impression."

Oh, *fuck*. I'm going to kill Micah. "No, that's not—"

She holds up a hand. "I'm not trying to rush you both,

Asher. I respect your decision to consider everything carefully. But how can he make an informed decision if he's never been here before?"

Dammit, I'm going to have to lie. "It's not that. I… he's not local. And he doesn't like being teleported, so when you factor in travel time, it's not that easy for him to get enough time away from work."

"Where does he live?" Mom asks.

"And what does he do?" Dad adds. If they weren't genuinely interested in the person they think I'm dating, I'd want to strangle them. Can't they tell this is all a big fake?

"He's a…" Blank brain, blank brain. My gaze lands on the kids. "…teacher. And he lives in…" Where do I travel to reasonably often that isn't that close? "…England. He's English." There, that should satisfy them.

"And he's not a demon?" Chloe asks, fascinated by the concept. She's only ever met one person who's not a demon: Lucifer Sam, our cousin Gideon's boyfriend.

"No, he's not."

"What is he, then?"

Whyyyyy are they asking all these questions? I shoot a glare at Micah, who's grinning like a smug idiot. "He's, uh, a hellhound. And he has brown hair and eyes and is very nice," I add before anyone can ask, sending a mental apology to my hookup of the other night, whose identity I seem to be borrowing.

"What's his name?" Grandmother asks, still smiling.

I take a deep breath and commit fully to this farce. "Garrett."

CHAPTER FIVE

Garrett

At eight on Saturday morning, I put down my mug of tea, push aside the plate bearing toast crumbs, and call Alistair. I've deliberately timed it to wake him in the middle of the night.

The line rings four times before connecting, and all I hear is a muffled groan.

"Alistair?"

"I hate you," he grumbles, his voice rough with sleep.

"Good morning! How's your life been lately?"

"Whyyyyyy do you hate me?"

I scoff. "You can't ask people questions like that, Alistair. They'll answer you, and the list is long."

He says something, but he's not speaking into the handset and I can't make it out.

"What was that?"

"Nothing. I was just waking Aidan so he can share in my pain."

I shake my head slowly in disbelief, even though he can't see me. "You woke your boyfriend for no reason? He's going to leave you if you're not careful."

"Never. He loves me too much." He's starting to sound more like his usual chipper self now.

Aidan's Irish lilt comes clearly down the line. "Not that much. Who is that and why do they want to be murdered?"

"It's Garrett. You like Garrett. Shhh."

"Sorry, Aidan," I call, feeling a little guilty. Aidan's a good man, and he *is* my species leader.

"Not to worry," he answers. "I know whose fault this is."

"Hey!" Alistair exclaims in an injured tone. "I was *sleeping*."

"So was I," Aidan says darkly. "What was it you needed, Garrett?"

"Information. There's a woman here who seems to have a lot of influence, and—"

"Gideon's grandmother," Alistair announces. "Is she as scary as everyone says?"

I blink. "You didn't think it might be relevant to tell me there was a scary, important person here so I could get some background and be prepared?"

Shrugs don't make sounds, but I can still tell my idiot cousin is shrugging. "You're a clever man, Garrett. I knew you'd be able to manage."

I pinch the bridge of my nose and count silently to ten. I should have left him at the park when he was an infant. My aunt would have been sad at first, but she'd have gotten over it. And he'd be some other family's problem.

"Tell me about her now," I order, as patiently as I can manage.

"I don't know much," he admits. "Sam's terrified of her. She tried to kill Andrew once."

"Andrew Turner? Who works with you?" I met him at our cousin Elinor's wedding, but I'd heard a lot about him before that—and not just from Alistair. He's almost as old as Damaris and is highly respected. "Why?"

"Who knows? He probably deserved it. Andrew can be so annoying."

I pull the phone away and stare at it. Is he really that lacking in self-awareness?

"Garrett?" his faraway voice says, and I put the phone back to my ear.

"So you don't know anything else about her?" I decide to ignore his earlier comment.

"Nope. I could ask Sam?"

Aidan clears his throat.

"Oh! Aidan knows her. I forgot that."

I swear, I don't know how he gets through the day.

"Aidan, could I impose upon you to slap Alistair?" The sound that comes down the line, followed by Alistair's howl of (fake) pain, is immensely satisfying. "Thank you."

"It was my pleasure," Aidan says sincerely. "Let me tell you about Damaris Bailey so I can get back to sleep."

I listen carefully as he runs through the highlights: immense family wealth, generations of influence, a history of looking after less fortunate demons. And that's just the Bailey family. Damaris herself was a soldier for a time, then an intelligence operative. She worked for the Community of Species Government for nearly a century in various roles, then sidestepped to focus on her family and various demon causes. People are afraid to cross her, but if they genuinely need help, she's the person they go to.

"'Genuinely' is the key word here," Aidan adds. "If you screw with her, try to take advantage, she'll end you. There have been people who mistook her generosity and kindness for softness, and those who lived through it still regret it."

That's… not reassuring.

"Great. Thanks, Aidan."

"Anytime. Good luck."

We end the call to the sound of Alistair whining about how he helped too and where was his thanks?

Now that I have more information, I can formulate a better plan. My objectives for the year are to (a) educate the children, (b) develop a working system to attract other species to the town, (c) make observations for my paper, and (d) avoid Damaris Bailey as much as possible.

I think I can manage that.

SDC

SID AND ANNIE hang back as I approach Damaris's house, and I glance over my shoulder at them. "What?"

"We're terrified of her," Sid says bluntly. "She's called six times in the past three days, and every time I hear her voice, my testicles try to climb back into my body."

I turn fully to face him. How to deal with this? "Why?"

Annie scoffs, not falling for my fake ignorance, and Sid shakes his head. "Instinct."

That surprises a laugh from me. "I'm not saying she's not intimidating"—that's as diplomatic a word as I can manage—"but she's been… polite to us."

"She hates our guts, Garrett," Annie says bluntly. "She doesn't want us here."

"She doesn't hate us," I argue. "Come on, we study this kind of behavior in people. We know what it means. We're outsiders, and she's not sure what to make of us yet." And she might also hate us. The vibe I've gotten from her over the past few days hasn't been promising. But I'm not going to tell my team that. "She's hosting this party to welcome us, right? So let's not insult her by being late."

They nod—reluctantly—and we close the distance to the front door and knock.

To all our relief, the demon who opens the door is not Damaris. He's a lot younger, for one—younger than me even—and even though he's not smiling the way a non-demon would, he *is* smiling. I don't even have to look closely to see it.

"Hi! I'm Zac Bailey, Damaris's grandson. And you're our teaching team. Welcome. Come in."

I smile at him as he stands back and holds the door wide. "Thank you. I'm Garrett Smythe." I introduce the others as we enter, and then look around as Zac closes the door. The murmur of voices comes from down the hallway, but it's the hallway itself that intrigues me. It's lined with pictures, dozens—no, hundreds of them. The ones nearest us are drawings and paintings, some of them clearly dating back a long time, while farther down the hall I can see sepia-toned photographs. They're all images of people whom I assume Damaris knows—or knew. "This is wonderful," I comment, stepping closer to study a water-color miniature. "Fascinating."

Zac comes to stand at my shoulder. "Yeah, Grand-mother's gallery is pretty cool. This is her younger sister. And that's my late grandfather's cousin." We move slowly down the hall with Zac identifying the subject of each framed image. The anthropologist in me is thrilled, wondering if Damaris would be willing to give me this same tour and maybe tell me a bit about the pictures. It would be grea—

"And this is Ezekiel Levin. Grandmother worked with him a long time ago. They loathed each other, and the story is that she killed him one day when he wouldn't take his feet off her desk. Nobody ever found his body." Zac's tone is completely unconcerned, conversational, even, just as it was when he told me about his grandfather's cousin. But Annie and Sid go silent, and my gut freezes. He can't be serious?

"Ah, ha ha. That's an… interesting story."

Zac shrugs. "Yeah, I've always liked it. Nobody could ever prove anything, of course." He moves on to the next image, leaving me blinking in shock and overflowing with questions.

The rest of the tour introduces a few other people Damaris supposedly hates, including Andrew Turner, Alistair's work colleague. I'm starting to feel edgy now, wondering if I'll make some stupid misstep and incite my hostess to murder me.

The big room we enter is full of people—some of them I recognize, like Jesse and the council members, but a dozen or so more are strangers to me. They're standing around with drinks in hand, chatting and mingling, and beyond them is a wall of windows looking out at the alps. The encroaching sunset paints the peaks in fiery colors, and for a moment I'm captivated by the stunning view.

"Dr. Smythe," a now-familiar voice says, and I drag my gaze from the vista to focus on Damaris. "I hope Zac's been looking after you."

I muster a smile. "Good evening. Your house is beautiful. Zac showed us your gallery—I'd love to speak with you about it sometime." Although preferably only with witnesses present.

She gives me nothing except a flat stare. "Come and meet some more of my family."

With Sid and Annie trailing three "safe" steps behind us, she introduces me to her son and daughter-in-law, her daughter, and her other son's girlfriend. They greet us warmly, but then as the conversation picks up, they take their cue from Damaris, and I start getting outsider vibes again. This is going to be a big problem. Damaris has a lot of influence in the village, and if she continues to make it clear she's not receptive to our presence and our research, others will also close us out. Lucifer Sam has asked me to help prepare the village for other species to move in, and I'm going to need Damaris's support.

I just need to find a way to get it.

"Is your other son here too?" I ask her. His girlfriend is, so I'm assuming he's around. Maybe I can win him over before Damaris can make her position clear, and he can convince her how awesome I am. Or something.

"He is. Somewhere," she says. "Oh, and meet another of my grandsons. Asher." She taps the arm of a tall demon with his back to us, and he starts to turn.

Something niggles in my brain. I'm looking at the back of his head, but there's…

His face comes into view, and my stomach flips.

It's my one-nighter from Zurich. Damn.

Oh, well. It's a little awkward, but we're both adults. Maybe he's the ally I need? I start to smile, prepared to make a joke along the lines of "fancy seeing you here," but his expression goes from pleasantly neutral to shocked—dare I say horrified?—in a split second.

"What are you doing here?" he gasps.

"Uh," I stutter, not sure what tack to take.

Damaris looks between us. "Do you know each other?" She draws in a sudden breath. "Wait… Garrett?"

I turn to her expectantly, waiting for her to finish her question, grateful for the distraction, but she's staring at Asher. "Is this your Garrett?"

His Garrett? Did he tell his family about me? After one night of casual sex where we didn't even exchange last names or phone numbers?

That's… disturbing.

"Well," he begins instead of immediately saying no, and she must take that as a yes, because she rounds on me with bright eyes.

"Why didn't you say? Oh, this is a wonderful idea! A trial year in the village to see how you like it, and you can help us fix everything the way you need it to be."

I swallow and desperately try to think of something intelligent to say, wondering what the ever-loving fuck he's told her. But then she frowns, her face turning stone-cold terrifying in an instant, and I have to fight the urge to step back.

"But Asher, you just asked Garrett what he was doing here. Did you not know…?" She looks between us again, clearly waiting for an explanation.

"This is amazing," I hear someone whisper behind me, but I'm too scared to take my eyes off Damaris to see who.

Fortunately, Asher chooses that moment to recover from his stupor. "Grandmother, I'll explain everything, but first could I have a moment with Garrett? Thank you." He doesn't wait for an answer, just takes hold of my elbow and hustles me toward a doorway. Annie and Sid stare at me wide-eyed as we pass them. They've never seen me in such an unprofessional moment.

The room we enter has a long dining table in it, but there are no people, and as soon as Asher closes the door, I round on him. "What the fuck is going on?" I don't usually swear when I'm working, but if ever a situation warranted it, this would be it.

"I'm sorry," he says immediately. "I'm so, so sorry. But I need you to pretend to be my boyfriend."

I play the words over again in my head as he watches me, no apology in his expression despite his words—and believe me, I'm looking hard for it. Instead, there's a combination of expectation and demand.

That just makes me mad.

"I beg your fucking pardon?" Whoops, there's that f-word again. Somehow, I'm okay with it, since my one-night stand who I never expected to see again is asking me to pretend to be his boyfriend… and his family seems to think I already am. The family I need to impress with my professionalism and capability.

"It's complicated. Really complicated. But if you pretend to be my boyfriend while you're here, I'll… I'll give you whatever you want. Pay any rate you want."

A thrill of… something runs through me. Surely not excitement. No, it's offense. I'm offended by his implication that I can be bought.

Not excited.

"I'm an anthropologist, not an escort," I hiss. "Why —*why* would you even ask this?"

He shrugs. "It was worth a shot?"

I stare at him. "It was…" Spinning on my heel, I head for the door, but he puts on a burst of speed and gets there before me, blocking it.

"Hear me out, please. I know this is weird, but… well, you've met my grandmother, right? Have you talked to her for more than two minutes?"

"Of course I have," I snap. "She's called me thirty times in the past three days."

"So you get it, then. You know how… determined she can be once she fixates on an idea."

I give him my best withering glare. "I very much doubt Damaris fixated on the idea of me being your boyfriend without even knowing that your supposed boyfriend was me!" I don't even think that sentence makes sense, but he gets the idea.

"That's really bad luck and stupid coincidence," he

admits. "Give me two minutes of your time, and I'll explain."

Folding my arms across my chest, I wait. Mostly because I'm super curious. Not because standing this close to him and inhaling his amazing scent is stirring memories of the other day and just how well we fit in bed.

"My grandmother is 973," he begins. "She's lived a long and full life, and she loves nothing more than her family."

I thaw somewhat. As scary as Damaris is, I can't deny that all her questions and concerns are based around doing the best for this village—including her family.

"She's decided now that she wants to see a new generation before she goes to the spiritual plane. She's already started a campaign of nagging my two cousins who have partners, but she also thinks the odds will be better if more people are trying… so to speak. And since I'm the oldest unattached grandchild, I'm the one she's putting the most pressure on to find someone special and embark on a life of domestic bliss and babies."

My arms fall away from my chest, but the stiffness of my posture remains. "Your grandmother wants you to meet someone and be happy, so you told her you were dating me?"

"No! I mean… yes." He frowns, and I resist the urge to step back. I don't know him all that well, but we've done unspeakable things to each other's bodies, and his whole family is in the next room. I'm fairly sure he's not going to hurt me, no matter how scary that frown is.

Unless that story about Damaris's coworker is true and Asher takes after his grandmother.

Pushing that lovely thought aside, I raise a brow and wait for him to elaborate.

"It's not just that she wants me to meet someone. She's

actively matchmaking. She invites people over when I'm here and tells me to pick one. The children and grandchildren of her friends have all suddenly started visiting Zurich and need me to show them around or keep them company. A few months back, one of them 'won' a Mediterranean cruise for two and needed 'a friend' to go with them. I'd never met this person in my life, and it was a couples' cruise!"

I can't help it: my lips twitch. He doesn't seem to notice, too caught up in his own drama.

"And then I got home yesterday, and she told me that she had a *mathematical* plan to find me someone. She wanted me to put together a list of criteria so she could find people that fit and take turns inviting them to meet me until I found 'the one,' like some stupid reality show that everyone knows is fake. How is that mathematical?" He sounds outraged as he says "mathematical," making me wonder if his distress is actually because of the matchmaking or just deep offense on behalf of the concept of mathematics. Maybe both. Finance people are weird that way. "Anyway, I was panicking, but I *didn't* tell her I had a boyfriend."

He didn't? "So why does she think you do? And why does she think it's me?"

CHAPTER SIX

Asher

"It's Micah's fault," I declare, throwing my cousin under the bus without an ounce of regret.

"Who's Micah?" he asks, looking confused in that exaggerated way non-demons do. It's adorable on his face, which I'm very fond of after seeing it contorted in ecstasy. Not to mention, the memory of his soft, puffy lips stretched around my cock is one I'll treasure for a long time. He gave me the hottest night—and day—I can remember in all my hundred and ninety-three years.

I force myself to focus. Maybe if I can convince him to help me out, we can negotiate the terms of our agreement to include more hot, sweaty, delicious sex. Though probably not if I use the words "negotiate," "terms," and "agreement."

"Micah's my cousin. He opened his stupid fat mouth while I was trying to think of a solution, and told everyone I couldn't participate in that stupid match-dating scheme because I'm seeing someone."

"He told your grandmother you were seeing me? How? I've never met Micah."

Fuck. This isn't going to go well for me. "No, he just said I was seeing someone. Well, he said I was seeing a non-demon who wasn't sure he could handle living in the village for at least part of the year, and that's why I'd kept it quiet. Because we're taking it slow."

He looks at me expectantly, clearly waiting for me to explain how that led to tonight's shitshow of Grandmother thinking he's my boyfriend.

Although, really… it's the perfect solution. He's here for a year anyway. And it's not like he'd be stuck with me all the time… I spend about half of every month in Zurich.

"People were asking me questions about my imaginary boyfriend," I continue, "and I… panicked. Your face popped into my head, and I didn't think I'd ever see you again—I definitely didn't think you'd ever meet my family —so I, uh, borrowed your identity. Sorry?"

He stares at me, unblinking, for a minute, then nods stiffly. "I suppose I can see how that would have happened. And I didn't expect to see you ever again, so maybe if I'd been in a similar situation, I would have done the same thing." He sounds doubting, and I'm sure he's judging me hard. But he doesn't say so or show it, and I'm grateful. I really don't need my hookups thinking I'm an idiot.

Although… given what I plan to ask next, that may still happen.

"It's just a stupid coincidence," I add. "Or…"

Wariness takes over his expression. "What do you mean, or?"

"Well… doesn't it seem an incredible coincidence that of all the people in Zurich, it was you, the one person who would be moving to my village and meeting my family, that I hooked up with the other day?"

"Not the one person," he corrects. "My team is here too. There are three of us."

I ignore that. It's not relevant and doesn't help my point. "And then, of all the people I've met in my life, and all the many combinations of people I could have made up, I used your name and description when my family asked about my fake boyfriend."

"It *is* very coincidental," he agrees slowly.

"Is it, though? Or is the magic taking a hand in things? It does that sometimes, you know." Or so Gideon, my cousin, tells me. His boyfriend is the lucifer, so he'd know. It seemed kind of farfetched to me that the existential magic that makes up the universe and selects our leaders would care about individual people.

Garrett's face changes to incredulous disbelief. I've always loved that other species have no subtlety of expression. It makes negotiating with them so much easier.

"Are you trying to say that this whole… whole… *debacle* was *fated*?" He looks like he's going to start sputtering at any moment, and affection rushes through me. I barely know him—except carnally—but already I like him.

I definitely like what he did to me when we were naked.

"I don't believe in fate," I scoff. "But I know the magic acts to make things happen that otherwise might not. Grandmother said the lucifer interviewed you personally—surely, after meeting him, you can concede that's true?"

He nods stiffly. "Alistair said it happens sometimes," he admits.

"Alistair?" Something clicks in my brain. "Alistair *Smythe*? Are you related?" I know of Alistair Smythe, of course. He works directly for the lucifer—with Gideon, believe it or not. Gideon's told me some stories that make me wonder how my chronically impatient cousin hasn't strangled him yet.

"He's my cousin."

I seize on that. "See? I didn't know that… how could that be yet another coincidence? Alistair works with my cousin Gideon—they're both the entire reason you're here. Would you have been in Zurich if not for them? No? They're the reason you and I met. It must be that the magic is taking a hand in this."

The disbelief morphs to pure skepticism. "To what end? Why would the magic want your grandmother to think I'm your boyfriend?"

I have no idea how to answer that, because the truth is, there's no possible way the magic cares about Grandmother's matchmaking scheme. So I have two seconds to make something up that sounds plausible and will convince Garrett that he should go along with this whole cocka-mamie plot.

"Maybe it knows that the village—and Grandmother —will behave differently, treat you differently, if they think you're family. Maybe it needs your anthropological view-point on what's happening here, but knows you'll only see what you need to if you're fully accepted from day one. Which you would be, as my boyfriend." Wow, that wasn't believable at all.

Oddly, though, he seems intrigued. Could he actually have fallen for it?

"It is a known phenomenon that people behave differ-ently with family and friends than they do with outsiders," he muses. "And your grandmother was much warmer toward me when she thought I was dating you."

"Yes, exactly," I agree, even though I don't see how it would make much difference. He's here to teach the kids and tell us what we need to do to make the village accessible and welcoming to other species. How would it make a difference to that if Grandmother invites him to weekly family dinner or not? "While you're here, we tell everyone you're my boyfriend. Then, toward the end of the year, we start acting like things aren't working out, and nobody will be surprised when we 'break up' and you go back home. You'll get what you need for your study, and I'll get a year's reprieve from Grandmother's matchmaking. Maybe more, since I can pretend to be heartbroken for a while after you're gone," I add, seized by inspiration. "Who knows, maybe she'll shift her focus to Micah this year and forget all about me." That would be amazing. Nobody deserves it more than him.

But Garrett's shaking his head. "I haven't agreed to anything yet," he cautions. "I don't like the idea of deceiving your grandmother. She's been…" He hesitates, and I get it. Grandmother is a lot of things, including kind, but it's not usually the first impression people get of her. She takes time to warm up to strangers.

"I promise she won't kill you," I assure him earnestly. I could probably stop her. And if not, well, he'll be dead. It's not like he'll be able to come after me for breach of promise.

I don't think he's entirely convinced, so I switch tactics. "We don't have to deceive her. We could be boyfriends for real."

He blinks three times and then says, "Are you on medication you've forgotten to take?"

"No, hear me out. We get along, don't we? And we're definitely sexually compatible. Why can't we be boyfriends?"

Taking a slow step back, he says, "You do know that what you're describing isn't a relationship, right? It's friends with benefits. Which still wouldn't apply to us, because we're not friends."

I fake hurt feelings. "We're not? I feel friendly toward you. Why would you say we're not friends?"

He rolls his eyes. "Stop it. I'm onto you now. You can't manipulate me this way."

Sighing, I drop all pretense and say, "I need this, Garrett. What will it take for you to help me?"

He purses his lips and studies me for a long moment. "I'm not insensitive to your plight," he begins, and I press my lips together to keep from smiling. His big, fancy words are so cute. He can't be that much older than me, but sometimes he talks so much more formally. "Unfortunately, I'm not comfortable deceiving your grandmother and everyone else by pretending we're boyfriends. If we're found out, it will greatly jeopardize the job I've come here to do. And the fact is, we can't really be boyfriends, because we're not."

My stomach sinks. Dammit. This is a disaster. Not only does it mean Grandmother will have free rein to continue her matchmaking, but I'm also going to have to admit to lying to her. And drag Micah into the line of fire with me.

The memory of what Sam, Gideon's boyfriend, suggested floats through my brain, summoned by my desperation. What did he call it… a MOC. Marriage of convenience. I've dismissed it as ridiculous, but… is it?

"Marry me," I blurt.

He takes a step back, shock written all over him. "*What?*"

"Let's get married. That will give you a position as part of my family, and Grandmother will go out of her way to make you feel welcome. It will definitely prevent her from trying to set me up with anyone else. And since we really will be husbands, you won't need to lie about it." It's the perfect solution.

"You can't be serious." He's staring at me like I'm insane, but… is that a tiny spark of interest?

Maybe I'm imagining it, but I push on anyway. "It would let us maintain this charade without the same degree of dishonesty. I get my year of reprieve—possibly more—and you get to work within this community as a family member. The only other way you could get that is for me to adopt you."

He doesn't laugh, dammit, but that spark is definitely there.

"What do you imagine the marriage would entail?" he ventures cautiously. "It sounds all shiny and perfect, but marriage is a legal commitment. I can't tie myself to someone I barely know without having some ground rules in place."

Yes! I resist the urge to fist pump, but I've got him now. He's shown interest in my proposition—all that's left is the negotiation, and that's my field of expertise.

"A business arrangement only," I assure him. "I can have the paperwork drawn up. We agree to marry, keeping all our assets separate, making no financial claim upon each other, for a minimum of one year or as long as both parties are happy to continue. For all intents and purposes, in the eyes of the world, we'll be married and will behave as such."

He nods slowly. "And, er… I understand demons have a ceremonial marriage ritual that takes place privately. Would we be taking part in that?"

What… an unexpected question. But given how casual he's trying to look, I'm guessing this is a big selling point for him. Which makes sense, him being an anthropologist and all. "Yes, if you don't mind. It would be hard to explain why we didn't. But it's a simple thing." Basically just a repetition of vows. Seizing the opportunity, I add, "There are some other ceremonies and rituals you'd need to attend as a member of the family, too. The autumn equinox and midwinter are the next two."

His eyes light up, and I'm pretty sure I've won. If he wants private demon rituals and customs, I'll dig up every single one I can think of. It's cute how excited he seems about it.

"What about sex?" he blurts, and my chest seizes. Does he mean…?

Reality crashes in on me. "We can have sex," I assure him, and then wince. "With other partners," I add hastily. "I'm not saying I expect you to… service me. But we would be allowed to pursue other partners. Discreetly." I shudder to think what my parents and grandmother would say if they found out I'd cheated on a spouse. I'd be better off admitting to the lie.

"No," he says flatly, then shocks me by adding, "a sexual relationship would be part of our marriage—for as long as both parties are happy to continue. Should that cease, terms of sexual activities with other partners can be negotiated. But if you're fucking me, you're not fucking anyone else."

I… wasn't expecting that, but fucked if I'm going to say no. I nod and clear my throat. "That seems… fair." More than fair. Amazing, actually. "So… are we really doing this? Getting married?"

He looks me in the eye and nods. "We're getting married."

CHAPTER SEVEN

Garrett

"And so, it's my pleasure to announce that Garrett and I are getting married," Asher declares to the room.

What have I done?

No, seriously, *what have I done?*

I don't think I can even blame him for this, since I didn't laugh in his face when he suggested marriage. But now, as the room erupts into exclamations of shock and pleasure, I can only assume I was temporarily insane. What other explanation can there be?

Not insane. Tempted by culturally significant customs.

Damaris finishes hugging Asher and turns to me, her face lit up with a smile even I can see. "Garrett, I can't say I'm not surprised, but I'm so happy," she says. "I look forward to getting to know you better. What made you decide so soon that the village is right for you?"

Fortunately, Asher swoops in to rescue me before I have to answer. "Come and meet my parents," he says, bodily pulling me away from Damaris. I shoot her an apologetic look, but she just waves me off, no doubt already thinking she can corner me later. Since I'm going to be related to her and apparently going to live here forever.

What have I done?

I push the thought aside and concentrate on not making an idiot of myself as Asher introduces me to his parents and his little sister, who's going to be one of my students this year. She looks up at me with big eyes. "Are you going to be my brother too now?"

"Yes," I reply. We'll have to work out the classroom logistics of this another time. "It's nice to meet you, Chloe." She beams at me and stands on tiptoe, beckoning for me to bend down.

"Will you shift for me?" she whispers.

I grin as I straighten. "Definitely," I promise. "We can play fetch." Don't judge me. Chasing stuff is fun.

She laughs delightedly, and Asher's answering smile is wide enough for me to see clearly. He obviously loves his sister.

Next, we're swept around the party, meeting people I hadn't been introduced to yet, accepting congratulations and dodging questions about when the wedding will be. We haven't had time yet to discuss details of this plot—Asher thought it would seem suspicious for us to be away from the party for too long, and he was convinced that a wedding announcement would distract from all the awkward questions for now. He wasn't wrong.

I'm increasingly aware of those who *aren't* celebrating with us. Sid and Annie look confused—as well they might, since as far as they knew, I was single, and they'd certainly never heard of Asher before. And Asher's cousin Zac is standing with another man who looks enough like Zac and Asher for me to guess he's probably Micah, and they're both watching us with an odd mix of amusement and suspicion.

"I need to talk to my team," I mutter to Asher when it seems as though we've made a full circuit of the crowd. Damaris is bearing down on us, and I figure he can deal with her questions while I try to smooth over this professional dumpster fire I've somehow managed to set.

"Go," he agrees, and I slip away to where they're standing off to the side. How to handle this?

"Congratulations?" Annie says as I approach, but it sounds more like a question than any kind of well-wishes.

"You're probably confused," I suggest. "This has been… somewhat of a whirlwind."

"Your personal life is your own business," Sid says. "A heads-up would have been nice, though. We didn't even know you were seeing anyone."

"Is that why you disappeared in Zurich? We wondered what you were doing," Annie adds.

"Yes." I seize on the excuse… which is actually the truth. "Asher and I spent the day together. And… I didn't actually know this town was his hometown. I-I…" Shit, can I make that work? It's the truth, but if I was really dating someone seriously—even if we were taking it slow—would I not know something like that? Especially if we were taking it slow *because* of his hometown's location.

This is getting complicated.

"I, uh, knew he split his time between here and Zurich, and I was hoping being in the area would give us more time together. And that living here would give me an idea of what things might be like in his village. Which turns out to be this one! So… surprise." I laugh weakly and then shut my mouth. I don't think I'm helping myself right now.

Surprisingly, they're both nodding. I guess they figure if I was going to make up a story, it would be a lot more believable than that. "Is this going to be a problem for the paper?" Sid asks seriously. "You being related by marriage to some of the subjects?"

Technically… yes. "I'll declare my bias, of course. But because it's purely observational research, it shouldn't be too big an issue. I'll understand if you prefer not to be associated with the project and want to return to England." Though it's going to leave me scrambling to find people to replace them… if I can even convince anyone to come, given I'm going to be marrying into one of the families I'm observing.

Holy crap, *what have I done?*

"No way," Annie says instantly, and Sid echoes her, sending relief flooding through me in waves. "We know your ethics, and we're not giving up the chance to work on such an interesting project."

I smile gratefully. "Thank you. I   "

"Garrett?" Asher appears at my side. "I'm sorry, I need to steal you for a moment."

"Uh, yes, sure. Have you met my colleagues yet?" I make hasty introductions, glad when Asher greets them both with interest and respect. They briefly exchange small talk, and then he makes our excuses and hustles me across the room. "What is it?" I murmur.

"My cousins. We need to talk to them."

I open my mouth to ask why, then abruptly remember that one of his cousins was the one who came up with the "he's got a boyfriend" idea in the first place.

The two men are waiting over by the window. Sometime in the last forty minutes they've gotten themselves drinks, and I find myself yearning for a good stiff drink. I definitely think I've earned it.

"Micah, Zac, this is Garrett," Asher says. "My idiot cousins, Micah and Zachary." He gestures to them in turn, even though I've already met Zac.

"Hello again," I tell him, and he laughs. Actually laughs out loud, in a most undemonic manner.

"Thank you," he says. "So much. Really. This has been one of the best nights of my life, and I think it's only going to get better. I sent a message to Gideon so he can also glory in this moment, but I don't think he's seen it yet."

Who's Gid—

"Oh fuck no!"

All three of them blink at me. "I beg your pardon?" Micah says politely, but all my focus is on Zac.

"What did the message say, exactly?" I ask, but in the next moment, my phone rings in my pocket… and so does Asher's. I groan.

"What?" he asks me.

"Alistair." And sure enough, when I pull out my phone, my cousin's name is on the screen. I contemplate ignoring it, but he'll just keep calling until I answer.

"Hello?" I answer as Asher rejects the person who's calling him—I'm assuming Gideon.

"You dark horse!" my cousin crows. "What secrets have you been keeping from me? Tell me everything now or I'll call your mother."

I hate him so much. "What makes you think she doesn't already know?" I bluff, smiling apologetically at Asher and his cousins—his *normal* cousins.

Well… almost normal, anyway. More normal than Alistair, that's for sure.

He hesitates for a second, then scoffs. "Nope. If she knew, I would have already gotten a call from *my* mother, asking why Aidan and I aren't engaged and why I didn't tell her you were seeing someone. As if I'm supposed to know everything you do."

Damn him, he's right. "We've been keeping it quiet," I hedge.

"Oh, *have* you? I don't know, Garrett. It seems awfully coincidental that you've been hot and heavy with a member of the demon family I just happen to have a connection with and who needs your help…"

Fuck, he knows. I think. "Hold on." I hit the mute button on my phone and look Zac in the eye. "What did that message say?"

He shrugs. "That Asher took the lucifer's advice and is getting married."

If Lucifer Sam gave Asher advice, Alistair probably knows about it. They're "bestest besties," as he likes to say.

I really should have done something about him when he was too small to fight back. The man's a tank now, and I don't think I'd win if I tried to take him down.

"What was the advice?"

Zac looks at Asher, and I snap, "Now, quick! Before he gets bored and calls the rest of the family!"

"It was about a marriage of convenience," Asher says. "The lucifer suggested I find someone agreeable and we marry in a business arrangement."

For a second, I'm so taken aback that I'm speechless. The *lucifer* suggested a marriage of convenience?

I shake off my shock and unmute my phone. "I know you know, Alistair. So stop harassing me. I have a lot of things to sort out right now."

My cousin makes a rude pfffft sound. "You mean like the details of your purely platonic, dull business marriage? Are you researching what marriage is like, Garrett? I'm so disappointed. I'm such a vibrant, interesting, lovable hellhound, and you're my cousin. How can you be so boring?" he teases.

I know perfectly well that I'm not boring—it's worth noting that Alistair once deemed base jumping "too boring for words"—so I scoff, then, just to get the upper hand, declare, "Actually, there won't be anything platonic about this marriage. Asher and I met three days ago, fucked each other into a stupor, and decided we want more of the same. Don't call me again today, Alistair. I'm busy. And don't you dare tell anyone else in the family, or I'll tell your mother you're thinking of proposing to Aidan and want her help planning it." I end the call on the sound of him spluttering. It's extremely satisfying.

"What, and I say this with all due respect, the actual fuck?" Micah breathes, and I suddenly remember the three demons standing with me. Who just heard me declare that Asher fucked me into a stupor.

I shake my head slightly. My life is normally so calm and ordered, people often don't believe I'm a hellhound. The events of tonight… this isn't my real life.

Still, no choice but to push on.

"Sorry about that," I say as breezily as I can muster. "You know what family can be like."

They all mutter agreement, and Asher furtively peers over his shoulder, skimming the room for signs that danger may be bearing down on us.

"So… Micah, right? It's nice to meet you. I'm Garrett." I stick out my hand, and he shakes it, eyeing me curiously.

At least, I think it's curiosity. It might well be gobs-macked awe that I can be so unhinged as to be in this situation.

"Nice to meet you too," he says. "Just… is your name really Garrett?"

"It really is."

His jaw drops, and despite the absolute fuckery of everything, I begin to enjoy myself.

Micah looks at Asher. "How…?"

Asher glances at me for permission, and I shrug. I

already told my cousin how we met; why shouldn't his know? Presumably, they're capable of keeping secrets.

"We really did meet three nights ago," he parrots what I told Alistair, "purely by coincidence. Neither of us knew about the connection until tonight. Last night, when I had to come up with a boyfriend on the spur of the moment, Garrett was still fresh in my mind, so…" He shrugs, then adds thoughtfully, "I didn't know he was a teacher, though. It's just a freaky coincidence that I said that."

That… really is a coincidence. For the first time, I give serious thought to the idea that Asher was right and the magic *is* interfering.

Micah looks between us. "So… what's going on?"

"Exactly what you think," I tell him firmly. "Asher and I have come to an agreement. I hope we can trust you to keep that to yourselves."

Their expressions visibly change, and even I can tell I've offended them.

"Of course they will," Asher intercedes. "And as soon as we come up with an official story, they'll confirm it."

"We will." Zac nods. "But in the meantime, Garrett, tell us about this stupor you and Asher fucked each other into."

Great. His family are just as annoying as mine. Who knew demons had a warped sense of humor… or any sense of humor?

"If your sex life is so lacking that you can't imagine the details yourself, I truly pity you. Don't worry, I'm sure we can find a sex worker willing to take you on." I sweep my gaze up and down his tall, fit form, then give him a mock pitying look. "Maybe if we pay triple their rate."

For a long, shocked second, all three of them stare at me.

And then they burst into loud, delighted laughter.

Heads turn, and faces relax into indulgent almost-smiles. It may take me some time to get used to living among demons, but I think I'm going to enjoy it.

CHAPTER EIGHT

Asher

I THINK Garrett may be planning to kill me and all my family.

Probably not *actually* kill, since he's a pacifist and a good, kind man. But metaphorically, I'm absolutely certain we're all dead and buried already.

Admittedly, I can understand why he might be feeling that way. Things have been a bit... intense. My grandmother is so excited that I'm getting married that she's determined to have the wedding as soon as possible. She cornered Garrett and demanded contact details for his family so they could start the planning immediately. It was only Garrett's firm insistence that he wanted to plan his own wedding—I have no idea if this is actually true or just an excuse—that slowed her down.

Then my dad showed up on his doorstep at the crack of dawn the next day to insist he spend the day with them so they could get to know each other. That led to an in-depth debate about our living situation... and whether he's "saving himself for marriage like the humans do."

That was a very awkward conversation that ended with

me threatening to put my parents in a human nursing home.

Then Garrett and I spent half a day hotly discussing the details for our marriage. It's fair to say that if this *was* a real relationship, we might have broken up after that.

None of this has been helped by my cousins, who watch and listen avidly and throw in the occasional inciting comment when it looks like things might be calming down. I'm pretty sure the only things keeping Garrett from going on a killing spree are a) the lure of demon cultural rituals, and b) sex. He came home with me after Grandmother's party, mostly because it would have looked weird if he hadn't, and we spent the night confirming that yes, we actually are dynamite in bed together. Some other parts of our relationship still need work, but not the sex.

Which means that two days after our surprise engagement announcement, I'm making careful notes of things I need to talk to Garrett about this morning. I figure if I write it all down—including my explanations and justifications—and stick to it, there's less chance of pissing him off. Maybe. I need him to agree to let me cover all his expenses while we're married. The school is paying for the house his team is staying in this year, and for the housekeeper who's looking after them, since they're not only here to teach but also to consult on attracting other species to the town. But their day-to-day expenses are their own responsibility, and I want to cover Garrett's. I know he thinks he's getting something out of this agreement, but it's not as much as I am.

Ideally, he'd move into my house, but I can see how it might be awkward with my cousins living there too and me away so much. We've decided to just wing it until the wedding and see if we can find an option that works for us. But whatever that turns out to be, I want to pay for it.

Garrett's a teacher and anthropologist; even if he's been very frugal with his income for a long time, he can't have that much money. I, on the other hand, could literally wipe my ass with thousand-franc notes for the rest of my life and still be stupidly wealthy.

I skim down the list one more time, then slip my phone into my pocket with a sense of satisfaction. This negotiation is going to go well.

♏

THIS NEGOTIATION IS NOT GOING WELL.

Garrett was in a shitty mood when he opened the door to me. Apparently he was on the phone to his mother and several aunts earlier, who have plans for "the wedding to end all weddings." He shut that down by threatening a courthouse wedding, but they somehow managed to extract a promise from him that they could host an engagement party for us.

Now he's pacing the limited floor space in the room designated as his office, muttering to himself about how it wouldn't have been *so* bad to have no family, surely, and maybe he could change his name and disappear. I don't bother trying to talk to him—he might be the most sensible hellhound I've ever met, but he is still a hellhound, and they're prone to high drama and silliness. He just needs to work it all off, and then we can have a sane conversation.

"This is all your fault!" he declares, rounding on me, and I blink.

"It… is?" I don't deny it, just in case that makes it worse, but I'm not sure how his family being hellhound-y and overbearing is my fault. Isn't it bad enough that I have to take responsibility for my own overbearing family?

"Yes! If you hadn't been in that bar with your wide

shoulders and your sexy scowl and your huge fucking cock, I wouldn't be in this situation. You owe me!"

Skipping over the fact that he was the one who approached me, I seize instead on the opportunity to change the subject and further my own agenda. "I do owe you," I agree. "I owe you so much. Let me make it up to you."

Suspicion flits across his face. "How?"

"Hmm, let me think… off the top of my head, I could pay some of your expenses. Groceries and incidentals, maybe?"

He stares at me. "What?"

Was that not clear? I thought it was pretty clear. "I'll set up an account for you, or if you prefer, you can keep the receipts and I'll reimburse you."

"Are you…? Do you really not get what I'm saying right now?"

I mentally replay his words. It's my fault and I owe him. That's it, right? I didn't miss anything?

"I owe you," I try, hoping for confirmation.

"Yes. You owe me for tempting me with your big cock." He says it slowly, and I get the idea that's relevant. I owe him… because he's attracted to me?

I glance through the office door into the hallway. Sid and Annie were leaving to set up the classrooms at the school when I arrived, and I haven't heard them come back. Still, I lower my voice as I say, "Could I maybe pay part of this debt with a blowjob?"

Garrett throws up his hands. "*Finally*, you get it."

Smirking, I stand and go to close the door. The last thing we need is for his colleagues to walk in on us. "You could have just asked, you know."

He sniffs. "We're getting married. You're supposed to be able to anticipate my needs."

I'm not touching that. Instead, I say, "Would you rather stand or sit?"

In response, he stalks over to his desk chair, spins it around, and plants himself in it. Then stands back up, opens his pants, shoves them down enough that I'll have clear access, and sits again. His eyebrows rise impatiently as he looks at me and then his crotch.

Laughing, I cross to stand before him, drop a kiss on his pretty lips, and then sink to my knees. "I'm sorry I failed to anticipate your needs. I'll try to do better." I close my hand around his rapidly hardening cock, and his breath catches.

"See that you do." He's trying to sound stern, but his lips are curling at the edges. I'm going to wipe away that amusement and leave him begging.

I settle back on my heels, lean forward, and take him as deep as I can. His hips jerk, and I gag and pull back.

"Sorry," he mutters as I wipe my mouth with the back of my hand. I meet his gaze.

"Don't be." But I lay one hand on his thigh to hold him in place. I don't mind choking on cock, but I want to be in control of it.

Garrett trembles slightly under my touch, and it's my turn to smile as I swallow his dick again. This time, I seal my lips as tight as I can around him and pull back slowly, so slowly, and his breath explosively leaves his chest. I pause at the bulbous head and work my tongue along the vein there. Then I do it all over again.

And again.

And when his breath is stuttering and his whole body is trembling, I switch things up and focus only on sucking the head. Garrett's hand lands on my head, fingers tangling in my hair. "Asher, please."

I pull off, panting. "What do you want?" His face is flushed and his pupils blown. I love seeing him this way.

"I want to come down your throat so hard that I see stars."

Not bothering to answer, I wrap one hand around the base of his cock and get back to tormenting the head with my tongue.

"Ashhherrr," he moans. I adjust my position slightly to take the pressure off my own dick, which is achingly hard in my pants, and then envelop every free inch of his cock with my mouth.

As if on cue, his barbs pop out, scraping gently along the tender inner flesh of my cheeks, and a second later Garrett explodes, cum filling my mouth and sliding down my throat. I swallow every bit I can before pulling off him and wiping my mouth.

His hand tightens in my hair as he looks down at me, both of us gasping for breath. "One minute, and then it's your turn."

CHAPTER NINE

Garrett

I'VE ALWAYS LIKED the first day of school when I'm teaching young children. The personalities and dynamics are fascinating. Some kids are excited, ready to take on any adventure that comes their way. Others are more timid, enthusiastic about the *idea* of school, but more reserved when it comes to the real thing. And some just don't want to be there.

There's so much to observe and learn.

This first day is extra special, though, because most of these children—and teenagers—have never met anyone who isn't a demon. In order to make things as stress-free as possible for the littlest ones, we asked that a family member be present for the first hour at least, to give some security while they get used to us. So far, though, things are going well. There are some kids hanging back and clinging close to parents, but most of the rest are mingling with each other and casting curious looks at me and my team.

The benefit of this being such a small community is that the kids already know each other. They've been playing together since they were infants, so there's no need for them to make friends—they already are friends. For those who've never been to school before, there's a new environment to become accustomed to, but otherwise, the only new or strange thing here is us.

Sid, who's been doing a headcount, gives me the nod that everyone is here. I step up to the front of the assembly room, where we asked everyone to meet, and hold up my hands. "Good morning! Could I have your attention, please?"

There's a round of shushes, but it takes a lot less time than usual for everyone to quiet down and look at me. They're all very curious about us, and I'm going to make that work in our favor.

"Thank you. Welcome back to school! I know it's been some time since you were able to be here, and we hope to make this a fun experience for you. I'm Garrett Smythe, and these are Sid Lane and Annie Adarsh. We're going to be running the school this year." We had an intense and occasionally heated conversation with Jesse and the council last week about how the children should address us. Some of the old guard—though surprisingly, not Damaris—wanted strict formality enforced. That's not my preference, though, and my experience backs it up, so I held firm to my plan, and as a result, the kids will be able to decide whether to address us by our given names or more formally. As I explained to the council, respect is inherent in the way one speaks, not the name one uses.

"You may have noticed that I'm a bit different from all of you. That's because I'm a canid shifter—or, to use the more common term, a hellhound. We'll have plenty of time throughout the year to talk about the differences between our species, but is there anything important you'd like to ask me now before Sid and Annie introduce themselves?"

I'm expecting hands to go up, and sure enough, they do. I pick one little boy who's leapt out of his chair and is hopping from foot to foot, waving his arm frantically. I know from reviewing the enrolment files that his name is Paul and he's seven years old.

"Yes, Paul?"

His mouth drops open. "You know my name? Is that a hellhound superpower?"

I bite back a grin. "No, somebody told me your name. Was that your question?"

He shakes his head vehemently. "My sister told me you can't teleport. Is she a big fat liar?"

A ripple of amusement runs through the adults, and among the teens, his sister, Megan, rolls her eyes and mutters to her friends.

"She's not a liar," I tell him, omitting the adjectives. "I can't teleport. Instead, I can change form into a canid—a dog."

Most of the older kids already know this, but many of the smallest ones gasp. I decide a demonstration might be the best way to move things along. I check first to make sure all the supervising adults are with their children, then shift.

Cries of startlement and delight ring through the room, and my hellhound self glories in the attention. I'm an average-sized hellhound, which is to say bigger than any other dog they would have seen. My coat is the same mid-brown color as my hair, and I stroll along the front of the room, letting them see me move. Turning to face them, I yawn, showing off my teeth, flick my ears, and leap up onto the table. The kids ooooh in delight, while the teens mutter about how cool it looks—which of course my hellhound hearing picks up. Our hearing and sense of smell are the sharpest of any species, something I'll be teaching them this year. Probably with some games of hide-and-seek.

I jump off the table and shift smoothly back to my biped form. "Any other questions?"

Three times as many hands go up this time, and I call on one of the older kids, a fifteen-year-old girl.

"Are you really marrying Asher Bailey?"

A hush falls over the room as all eyes turn to me. It's not a secret, so I'm not surprised she asked... or that everyone seems to know. But the almost reverent eagerness and interest with which they're waiting for my reply *does* surprise me. Sure, Asher is handsome and wealthy and dynamic, and his family is one of the most influential in this settlement... but do people really care so much that he's getting married? Even children?

Apparently.

"I am," I say, only to be bombarded with a flood of questions. Voices all jumble together, but my ears pick up "when?" "how did you meet?" and "will the wedding be here?" before I decide to tune them all out.

I raise my hands in a bid for quiet and wait patiently. Eventually, everyone falls silent, waiting to hear what I'm going to say. I study the sea of faces, looking for the subtle differences in expression that will tell me what they're feeling.

"I'm sure there will be plenty of time and opportunity for you to hear about my wedding to Asher," I offer. "Right now, I'm here to run the school. I think it's time to meet Sid and Annie."

Annie steps forward first. We conferred extensively with the village council about how she could demonstrate her abilities to the children. As a succubus, most of her talents are passive—she feeds off sexual energy, which is a simple thing to do in a town full of adults. Nobody would even notice it was happening. The more demonstrable of her abilities are defensive—low-key mind control powers. In modern society, incubi and succubae rarely need to use those skills, and many of them have morphed their talents to *giving* emotional boosts. In Annie's case, with the full consent of all students or parents, she can engender a feeling of positive competence during tests or soothe frustration and promote calm when a student is struggling to understand something. Annie's always careful to explain what she's doing before she does it, so the students understand those feelings are a temporary boost—similar to mood-altering medication, but without any side effects.

I observe the room carefully as she introduces herself and demonstrates her gift. The youngest students don't really seem to notice, but the parents and older kids do, and despite the concerns of the council, there's no fear or anger. This is going even better than I'd hoped.

Sid's introduction and demonstration are well received, as I expected. He's used to working with small children, and his sorcery talent includes the ability to manipulate light, so he gives silent, colorful miniature fireworks displays that are completely safe and don't stink up the room with smoke. It's always popular, and the whole room is oohing and ahhing and applauding when he's done.

I give them a moment to settle, then take command of the room again, reiterating the schedule for the school day and sending the kids to their classrooms. Primary-age kids are in one room, with Sid as their teacher, and the teens are in another, instructed by Annie. I'll be floating between rooms, helping when things are busy and overseeing when necessary.

As people start filtering out, I notice a small crowd clustered near one of the doors. My gaze snags on one head in particular: Asher. Even from behind, I'd know him anywhere… now. But what's he doing here? His mother came to reintroduce Chloe to the school, and his aunt is here as well, with her son Isaac.

I head in that direction. Whatever he's doing, it's distracting people and may disrupt classes. That's not acceptable.

He sees me coming and smiles. Not a smile designed for me to be able to see, but even after only ten days, I'm much better at reading demon expressions, and he's definitely smiling. There's also a distinct glimmer in his eye that makes me remember the way he wrung every last drop of energy from my body last night, fucking me until I couldn't have said what my name was. Including sex in our agreement was one of the smartest things I've ever done. The man is immensely talented.

"Hi," he says, his voice stroking over me like a caress. "I missed you this morning. You were gone before I woke."

Acutely aware of all the listening ears, I hasten to cover the last few feet between us so he can lower his voice. "I had a lot to do for the first day."

"Hmm, but I was hoping—" He cuts off abruptly when I give him a death glare, then smoothly says, "I was hoping to make you pancakes for breakfast."

One of the nearby parents chuckles. "I bet you were."

Asher pauses in leaning toward me to turn a cold stare on the man. "I beg your pardon?"

The parent takes a quick step back. "Nothing. Have a nice day." He grabs his kid and hastens toward the elementary classroom.

"Nice trick," I say dryly as Asher's gimlet gaze follows the man.

"Nobody gets to speak disrespectfully about you," he mutters.

"Then don't give them the opening to." If he thinks he's not at fault, I'll happily disabuse him of that notion.

I'm so busy mentally composing the lecture I plan to give him that I don't notice him leaning toward me—again—until his lips land on mine. I jerk back so fast, I almost overbalance. It's only my shifter reflexes that keep me upright.

"What are you doing?" I hiss, darting a glance around the room. There are still plenty of people here, and some of them are watching avidly. There's no chance they didn't see us kissing in my workplace.

My reputation for professionalism is going out the window.

"No kiss?" he asks. "We're getting married. People know we kiss."

"That doesn't mean you can kiss me in my place of work." I fold my arms across my chest. "Why are you even here?" He planned to go back to Zurich sometime today, since he's been here for ten days already. I'm still not sure if I'm grateful for the space that will give me, or if I'll miss him.

"I wanted to show my support."

Okay, I'll miss him. That's sweet. We still don't know each other that well, but I'm starting to like him. We've argued a lot this past week, but it's not nasty. We're just trying to learn about each other and plan a life together under stressful circumstances and in a short timeframe. It makes sense that emotions are running high… well, mine are, anyway. He seems to always be remarkably calm for a demon. Or maybe I'm just learning to read him better. I can tell the difference between his real frowns and his neutral thinking expression now, which means there are fewer times when I fear death by dismemberment in his company.

"I appreciate that," I concede, laying my hand on his arm and letting it rest there for a moment. It's the closest I'll come to showing him affection at work. It's bad enough everyone seems so excited and interested about our forthcoming marriage. I don't want them gossiping about my behavior as well. "What time do you need to go?"

He glances at the wall clock. "Soon. Now, really. I have a meeting at ten that I need to prepare for." He meets my gaze. "I was thinking... I have a dinner tonight, but tomorrow night I might come back? If you don't mind."

Why would it matter if I... ohhhh. Of course. If he's here, people will expect him to spend time with me. And everything I've heard indicates that he normally doesn't teleport back and forth each day, choosing instead to stay in Zurich for whole weeks at a time.

So what he's really asking right now is if I want to see him tomorrow night.

"That sounds nice," I say brightly, as though he offered to bring home pizza for dinner instead of fuck me all night. At least, I *hope* that's what's on offer.

His subtle smile comes and goes so fast, I'm not entirely sure it was there at all. "Good. I'll look forward to it." His gaze intensifies as he leans toward me, and suddenly my lungs seem too small for my chest...

Then he steps back, and disappointment crashes through me. I didn't want him to kiss me at school, of course. But now that he's not going to... I totally want it.

"Have a good day," he murmurs and is gone before I can think of a reply.

I suck in a breath and glance around to see how many people just witnessed me practically swoon at a mere look from my fiancé. This marriage may end up being less convenient than I thought.

CHAPTER TEN

Asher

Two Months Later

'This marriage is the furthest thing from convenient that I can think of.

Staring out the window at the gorgeous peaks of the alps, I wonder why I ever thought this would solve my problems. It's just given me a different set. The only thing good about it so far has been Garrett. Garrett in my bed, with his muscled frame that can handle anything I want to dish out. Garrett's sly sense of humor, making me see the funny things in even the most irritating moments. Garrett's inner hellhound putting in an appearance when I least expect it... cuddling beside me while I work at night, hiding my socks and laughing as I fail to find them, nagging me to play tug-of-war with him. Garrett's sensible professor side getting embarrassed when Micah walked in on us playing tug-of-war. Garrett fussing when he realized all the extra teleporting I've been doing to come home to him instead of staying in Zurich has resulted in me losing weight.

Keeping Garrett forever is something I'd seriously

consider. But this wedding is making me feel stabby. I finally understand why Gideon is always on his last nerve… it's the hellhounds.

Not Garrett, of course. His hellhound side is adorable. But his family… Yeah, I wouldn't be sad if something happened to prevent them from ever being able to contact us again. Especially since they're bringing out a side of Grandmother that's causing everyone to walk on eggshells.

Don't misunderstand: we all know Grandmother scares the shit out of other people. She even intimidates us sometimes. And we've heard the stories about how she deals with people who annoy her. But she's never been like this before. Garrett's mother called her to talk about the wedding, and halfway through the call, Grandmother threw the phone through a window and teleported out of Hortplatz. Nobody heard a word from her for the rest of the afternoon, but when she came back, she was spattered with blood, her knuckles were all grazed up, and there was this tense gleam in her eye that had us all backing away fast. Not that we think she'd hurt us, but…

We're still not sure where she went, but a few days later it was all over the news that an entire criminal organization in Geneva had vanished. Just… disappeared, leaving nothing but some smears of blood behind. Authorities are baffled. Nobody wants to ask Grandmother if she knows anything about it, but it seems like a big coincidence….

Since then, we've been trying to keep her away from the hellhound side of the wedding planning. Garrett had a long, very loud talk with his family about not calling her. Micah, Zac, and I sat outside and listened. He made a lot of threats, then finished with "As much as I wish you'd all disappear, I don't want the only thing left of you to be a bloodstain and an unsolved mystery."

My Garrett is so sentimental.

"Asher!"

As if on cue, he yells for me from the other room, and I hear stomping footsteps coming toward me. Sighing, I turn away from the window and wait for him to find me. It won't take long—his hellhound senses are amazing, and it's not like I'm trying to hide.

He appears in the doorway and glares at me. "I don't appreciate this, Asher."

I really don't want to ask, but I do anyway. "Don't appreciate what?"

"*Feeling* like this all the time. I'm grumpy, Asher. That's not normal for me. I'm the calm, rational member of my family. I'm the black sheep. The one they worried about because I was so subdued and never expressed my emotions at the top of my voice."

Nodding, I say, "I've noticed that about you. Normally hellhounds make me crazy, but you're very soothing."

It was the wrong thing to say, I realize as he snarls and launches himself at me with fingers hooked into claws. I guess I should consider myself lucky he didn't shift—

Oops, spoke too soon.

I duck and sidestep as he shifts midair, and manage to avoid having the entire weight of an adult hellhound plow into me. As it is, he knocks me off-balance, and I know I'm going to have a bruise where we collided.

I could have teleported completely out of his way, but if I had, I would have been too far away to grab hold of him. Wrapping my arms around his torso, I bury my face in the fur at his neck and hope fervently that he's not mad enough to actually use his teeth and claws.

"Love how soft your fur is," I croon, rubbing my cheek in it as I squeeze tight. He's wriggling to get free, but I'm not stupid enough to let go. As long as his claws remain sheathed, I have the advantage right now. "I'm sorry people are so stupid. Want me to rip someone's head off? I can do it, you know. You've been making me eat extra protein lately, and I'm super jacked."

He stills, possibly in shock. Or maybe he's thinking about it and mentally composing a list.

"Is it one of my cousins who upset you? Or both? I can definitely rip their heads off... or if you want to take a shot, I can hold them down and you can rip off an arm or leg."

His tense muscles relax, and he chuffs, then shifts back. I've never been so close to a shifter in the moment of their shift, and I freeze, not wanting to accidentally fuck it up and cause him to lose a limb. Is that even possible? It takes only seconds, and then my arms are full of warm, sexy Garrett in his biped form.

"You're an idiot," he mutters, turning to face me and burying his face in the side of my neck. He does that a lot, and when I teased him about being part vampire, he said it's because there's a concentration of scent there, and he likes how I smell.

"Why?" I ask, tipping my head to rest against his. "Because I want to avenge you against whoever doesn't appreciate you?"

He snorts a laugh, then lifts his head. "You can't just go around ripping people's heads off because they irritated me."

I look him dead in the eye. "I absolutely can."

"You're an investment banker," he argues. "Not a commando."

That's true, and admittedly, I don't have all that much experience ripping limbs off people... or even hitting them, unless you count pounding on my cousins when we were younger.

Speaking of cousins... "I can always call Gideon to

help. He's a commando... I think." The truth is, I don't know exactly what Gideon has done in some of the jobs he's had over the past century or so. Since he went to work at CSG nearly sixty years ago, his role has been a little clearer, but I don't think you get hired to work personally with the lucifer unless you have some very specific experience. He's the cousin who's most like Grandmother, which makes sense, when you consider how often she used to dandle him on her knee. He was the youngest of our generation, and she definitely spoiled him the most. We thought she was just reading him stories, but maybe she was actually training him to become a killing machine.

Do I really want to be the one who unleashes that on the world? "Or we can handle our problems in a nonviolent way."

Garrett sighs and smiles. It's small and tired but genuine, and I resist the urge to cuddle him closer and kiss him. He probably wouldn't appreciate it right now. "That sounds more like us. I analyze things and try to reason with them, and you throw money at them, then threaten them financially."

My jaw drops. "I do *not* threaten people financially."

The disbelieving look he gives as he steps back out of my arms is accompanied by a very dry "Oh, really?"

"Yes, really!" I'm offended that he even thinks that. I happen to be a highly skilled and respected investment banker, a financial expert people *beg* for guidance, and—

"So when Archie Webber asked if I had hellhound enthusiasm in bed, you didn't tell him it would be a shame if his nest egg broke?"

I clench my teeth tight together as residual anger from the memory trickles through me. Damn. I didn't know he'd heard about that. He *shouldn't* have heard about that. "That wasn't a threat. It was a… theoretical exercise. Archie's very philosophical."

This time, Garrett laughs out loud, and the sound of it makes me happy. I've gotten very attached to him, I can admit it, but it makes total sense. We're sexually compatible, get along well on most other levels, and he's meeting needs I didn't even know I had. Aside from the drama with the wedding planning, all the stresses in my life have lifted since he came into it, and as soon as we're safely married, the wedding stress will be over too. Keeping Garrett happy has become my number-one priority, because when he's happy, my life is better.

"How did you know about that anyway?" I ask, trying to sound casual and not like I'm planning to threaten whoever told him.

He gives me an arch look and says, "I have my ways. Don't think you can keep secrets from me."

It's ridiculous that I'm turned on by that, but I am. A completely nonsexy warning makes me want to throw him down on the bed and rip that sweater vest right off.

Speaking of nonsexy… how is it that I find him so desirable when he wears clothes like that? I've always been attracted to stylish, sharply dressed men and women. The middle-aged-suburban-dad-slash-professor look doesn't do it for me… or so I thought.

I take a step toward him, and he narrows his eyes. "If you think we're fucking before we resolve this, you're about to learn whether or not demons can grow their dicks back after they're cut off."

Instinctively, I suck in a breath and cup my crotch. "I thought we decided not to be violent?"

"Problems first, then sex," he promises. "Believe me, I don't want to hurt your cock any more than you do."

"Then why are you threatening it?" And why do I find

that hot? His assertiveness, not the threat to cut off my commando.

"Pay attention, Asher. I'm not happy."

That gets my full attention. Garrett needs to be happy, and I'll do whatever it takes to make that happen. "What happened?"

He sighs and sits on the edge of the bed. "I don't think we can have the wedding here in Hortplatz."

I wait for the part that's causing problems, but he seems to be done. "Okay." Garrett looks at me. I look back. "Are you going to tell me what happened?"

Those pretty brown eyes narrow again, and I resist the urge to protect my crotch. "Aren't you listening?"

"Yes," I assure him quickly. "You don't think we can have the wedding here. And honestly, I agree. The logistics of getting your family here, especially if teleporting makes them sick, are too complicated. And some of them are going to want to stay for a while, so we'd need to find room…. I'm not sure the village is big enough to hold an influx of hellhounds. Plus, there's no guarantee the weather will hold out. It would be terrible if we went through all the hassle of getting people here and planning the event, and the first blizzard of the season ruined it." I shake my head, remembering the times that's happened in the past. Autumn is a tricky time for any event up here. In winter, we can plan for sleds and snowshoes, but in autumn it's harder to tell what we'll need. Grandmother surprised us all by suggesting we wait for next summer, but Garrett and I both agree that it's better to get married ASAP and solidify his position in the family.

Plus, he really wants to be part of the demon wedding ritual.

"We should have the wedding in England," I suggest.

"It's far easier for my guests to teleport there than it would be for yours to travel anywhere else."

He blinks slowly at me. "I am going to kill you."

"Why?" I thought I was *helping*. I'm being reasonable and accommodating.

"You didn't think it would be a good idea to suggest this at any time over the past month while we've been trying to arrange the logistics of having the wedding here?"

Oh. He might have a point. It's probably not a good idea to say I haven't been paying that much attention to the actual details of the wedding planning.

"I thought you wanted it here, and I want you to have what you want," I say quickly.

He scoffs as he stands. "Nice try." Then, just as I'm wondering if I should run, he leans in to kiss me lightly. "But at least that's settled. You get to tell your grandmother."

I stare after him in consternation as he strolls to the door. "You're going to drop that and leave? I don't even get sex to soften the blow?"

Garrett glances back over his shoulder, and the tension from before is gone. There's a wicked gleam in his eye. "I'll give you as many blows as you want later."

I laugh as he leaves. That's more like it.

CHAPTER ELEVEN

Garrett

I GLANCE HURRIEDLY at my phone screen before I shove it back in my pocket. I'm waiting for Asher to message me that he's spoken to his grandmother so I can call my mother and get her started looking for a location for the wedding. I already know where I want to have it, of course, which is why I'm going to give her a very long list of requirements. She'll feel like she's involved and has achieved something when she comes back with the only possible place that fits, and I'll get what I want without having to justify it to her and listen to her suggest that we look at thirty other places first.

Family is hard work.

Asher hasn't texted, so I need to practice patience and concentrate on my task for the morning, which is introducing the half dozen five-and-six-year-olds at the school to shifters. I stick my head into Sid's classroom, and he pauses whatever he's saying to the older kids.

"Let's say hi to Garrett," he prompts, and there's a ragged chorus of "good morning" and "hello." I don't bother to hide my smile. Children delight me.

"Good morning," I say cheerfully. "Are we having a good day?"

There's another chorus of yeses, then one boy adds, "It's going to snow again tonight."

I try not to show my distaste for that. Zac said the same thing at breakfast this morning, and when I asked how he could be sure—the sky is a clear, glorious blue—he just smirked and said, "You learn to tell these things up here."

It's not that I'm against snow—I love a good snowball fight just as much as any other hellhound—but it's already snowed three times, and it's only mid-October. Sure, I know it snows a lot up here and the village gets cut off and all the rest, but facing the reality of it isn't as easy as the theory.

For starters, it's cold.

I thought I'd actually be able to make use of my fall wardrobe, but most days, I want to skip right to the winter clothes. Maybe we can use the lure of an early ski season to attract non-demons to the village. We need some kind of hook or attraction; something to differentiate this place and diminish the big honking negative of the isolation. Maybe the snow could actually be good for something.

"Snow. Yay," I manage, but I must be really unconvincing, because not even these primary-aged children look like they believe me. "Well," I say, trying to rally, "let's not disturb Sid's lesson any more than we need to. I believe some of you are coming with me?"

There's a little cheer from some of the smallest ones, and they scramble out of their chairs. Some hop from foot to foot, and I put a bathroom visit on the agenda. They might just be excited, but with little kids, it can be hard to know for sure until it's too late.

Sid and I both do a headcount to make sure everyone who's supposed to come with me is ready, and then I lead

them out of the classroom and into the assembly hall…
with a stop at the restrooms.

When we're all sitting cross-legged in a semicircle on
the floor, I say, "What do we know about shifters?"

All six hands go up, including Isaac's, Asher's littlest
cousin. We go around the circle.

"They can change into animals!"

"They can't teleport 'cause they shift instead."

"There are *two* kinds."

"They're kitties and puppies and would maybe be fun
to pet."

I make a mental note to spend some time on the
concept of not touching strange animals without permission. It wouldn't be so bad if it was a shifter—though it's
considered rude—but random dogs and cats can be
dangerous.

"Lucifer Sam is a kitty shifter."

"They poop glitter!"

My jaw drops, and I blink in shock a few times. We *poop
glitter?* As the other children ooh and aah and ask Isaac
how he knows that, I try to get my composure back. I
would have thought that he, of all the kids, would have
been the least likely to say something like that, since I've
had the most interaction with him and Chloe. They also
spent several days with Lucifer Sam. Clearly reality went
off the rails somewhere.

"Let's all settle down, please." I wait until they're quiet
again, then continue. "It sounds like you all know lots
already, but there's still more to learn. And I'm sorry to tell
you, shifters don't poop glitter." I can't believe that's a
sentence I had to say.

"Awww." The disappointed moan runs around the
circle, but Isaac sets his jaw.

"My brother Micah said they do." He sniffs. "Micah wouldn't tell a lie."

I highly doubt that, since it was Micah who told the lie that led to my engagement, but I'm not going to be the one to tell Isaac that. "Is that exactly what he said to you? He said 'shifters poop glitter'?" I've worked with enough kids to know things get mixed up really easily.

Doubt flitters across his little face, so like his brother's and cousins'. "Zac said Asher is sessed with you and he didn't know why, and Micah said you pooped glitter 'cause hellhounds love glitter."

The only part of that I can make sense of is that hellhounds love glitter. That's true. Even I'm susceptible to glitter-phoria, and I'm considered a low-key hellhound. But the rest… I'm not even sure what "sessed" was supposed to be. I really hope it's "obsessed" and not "sexed up" or something like that.

Regardless, the kids are all way too invested in this now, and I'm not going to get anywhere unless we settle it. So I pull out my phone. "How about I ask Micah to come and join us and explain exactly what he meant? Because I know that I for sure don't poop glitter. And then after that, we can talk about some other shifter things, and then play tag."

Little faces light up. "Play tag?"

I compose a quick text to Micah, using a lot of capital letters and exclamation marks. "Yep."

"Will you be a puppy when we play tag?" The question has a lot of anxious longing behind it, and I bite back a smile.

"I guess that depends on how the rest of the lesson goes. Now, let's talk about the two kinds of shifters."

It takes less than ten minutes before Micah puts in an

appearance, wearing a sheepish expression. I don't feel bad for what I'm about to do—doesn't know why Asher might be obsessed with me, huh? How about because I'm obsession-worthy?

"Say hi to Micah, everyone," I prompt, and the kids twist around to see him, shouting their greeting. I guess they're excited to hear the glitter poop story.

"Hi, kids," Micah says, coming to stand beside me and hovering awkwardly when I don't get up. Instead, I pat the floor.

"Join us, Micah," I encourage. "We don't bite." The kids laugh, and Micah sinks awkwardly down and tries to fold his legs the way we have ours. I guess it's been a long time since he's done this.

The smile he sends my way is apologetic and slightly afraid. I smile back with as many teeth as I can manage, and he winces.

"There's a little bit of confusion," I begin. "Isaac heard you say that shifters poop glitter, and as a shifter, I know that's not true." I mean, not without having ingested it first, which has happened on occasion for various reasons that I'm sure made sense at the time. "Could you help us clear this up?"

He swallows hard and looks at the six little faces watching him so intently. "Do I have to?"

"Oh, I really think you do." There's a slight edge to my voice now, and he nods slowly.

"Well… uh, what was it you heard, exactly, Isaac?" he stalls.

Isaac repeats what he told me, finishing with, "It's true, right? You wouldn't say it if it wasn't."

Micah actually begins to sweat, and I find myself enjoying this moment. "Well, it's not exactly true," he hedges, and there's a round of little gasps from the kids. They're so cute.

"You told a lie?" Isaac looks devastated.

"Not exactly." Micah sits there with his mouth open, as though trying to find the words, then looks at me for help.

I step in, but only because I can't stand the betrayed expression on Isaac's little face. "Micah, tell me if I get this wrong, but were you maybe joking with Zac? And because you know Zac already knows for sure that shifters don't poop glitter, you knew he wouldn't think it was true. Which makes it a joke, not a lie."

He nods frantically. "Yes. That's exactly what happened." He turns back to Isaac. "If I'd known you heard me, I would have explained why it was funny." There's a tiny wince with those words, and I guess he's thinking the same as me: if you have to explain it, it's not funny.

Isaac looks unsure. "So there's no glittery poop?"

Micah and I shake our heads in unison. "Sorry, buddy," he says. "Shifters can do some other really cool stuff, though. And hellhounds plan the best parties. Maybe Garrett will throw a party for you."

Any sympathy I was feeling for him is gone as the kids hype themselves up over a party I now have to plan. "You may talk quietly about shifters for a minute while I say goodbye to Micah," I announce, rising and yanking him to his feet with a steely grip on his arm.

"Uh-oh," he mutters under his breath.

As the kids start chattering—not quietly, but then, I didn't expect that—I drag Micah over to the door. "What is *wrong* with you?" I hiss. "Haven't you caused me enough trouble today?"

His expression turns sheepish. "Sorry? In my defense, I had no idea Isaac was listening."

"Kids hear everything. And what even did you say? You and Zac don't know why Asher's with me?" I've gotta say, that hurts. I thought we got on well. Also, they know exactly why Asher's with me, so being surprised that he's also attracted to me is… ouch.

"No, it wasn't… He only heard part of the conversation," Micah defends. "And he took it out of context."

"Well, he's five, so that sounds about right." I fold my arms and wait for him to explain it to me.

He looks like he might be about to teleport unexpectedly out of here to some random far-off destination. "It's just… Asher is… He's never…"

The volume rises on the kids' chatter, and I glance over. They're getting restless. "Go," I tell him. "I need to get back to work."

The relief that crosses his face is so obvious, anyone could have seen it. "Sorry about…" He waves his hand toward the kids. "And we're really glad you're here." He teleports out before I can respond, and I shake my head, trying not to be mad. There's no need to be, after all. I'll just tell Asher about this later and let him make his cousins squirm.

This whole marrying-a-demon thing has definite perks. I knew they were overprotective and possessive but didn't realize how much until Asher started glaring at people who talked to me for too long. From an anthropological perspective, it's fascinating.

From a personal perspective, I'm surprised by how much I like it.

Rejoining the kids, I settle them down, and we go around the circle again, talking about the differences between demons and shifters. I'm surprised by some of the questions they ask, but in the context of them never having seen or known about other species until recently, it does make sense.

"What's your puppy called?" Susannah asks earnestly.

I smile at her. "Garrett. We're the same person, just with two different forms. This is my biped form." I gesture to my humanoid body. "It's called biped because in another language, *bi* means two and *ped* means feet. I have two feet in this form, but in my canid form, I have four."

"Ohhhhh," they chorus, and predictably, a few of them look down at their own feet.

"Does that mean we're biped too?" Isaac asks, and I nod.

"Yep. All of us in the community, and humans too, are bipeds. That just means we have two feet that we walk around on. But when shifters change into our other forms—"

"You're not bipeds anymore!" Susannah shouts, the excitement of understanding clear in her voice. "What's it called when you have four legs?"

"Quadruped, but we don't call ourselves that," I add quickly. I'm pretty sure the long word will trip them up anyway, but it's better to move past the irrelevant info fast. "Do you remember what a shifter like me is called?"

"Hellhound," some of them say, and I nod.

"That's right, and there's a really fun story why we're called that. But remember I told you we had a different name before?"

A few small faces screw up as they try to remember, but one hand shoots up. "I know! Canis!"

"Canid," I correct, pairing it with a smile. "That's right. Excellent remembering. Dog shifters like me are called canid shifters, and we have a biped form and a canid form. And cat shifters like Lucifer Sam are called—"

"Felid shifters!" two of the kids yell in unison.

"Exactly right. And they have a biped form and a felid form. Now… I'm going to change, and you can see what I look like in canid form. After that, we'll play tag. But first, there are some rules we need to talk about." I run down the rules about where they can pet me, why it's rude to pet without permission, and how the game of tag will go.

I love my job.

<hr>

CHAPTER TWELVE

Asher

<hr>

I LOOK up from my desk as the buzzer in the outer office sounds. My assistant is working from home today, so I get up and go see who it is. I'm not expecting anyone—truth is, I'm rarely expecting anyone. I have the office purely to keep home and work separate, but it's not like I have clients or anything. My whole job is making money for my family and the village of Hortplatz, with the occasional favor for a friend thrown in.

When I see Micah through the glass outer door, my heart stutters in my chest. Why is he here? Has something happened? It's been less than two hours since I got here, and I spoke with Grandmother this morning. Surely they would have called… unless it's so bad the news has to be given face-to-face. I close the distance to the door in two fast steps, wrenching it open.

"What is it?" I gasp, and he pulls a face.

"I'm an idiot."

While that sinks into my brain, he pushes past me and wanders toward my office. Since there doesn't seem to be an emergency, I take my time closing the door and following, giving myself space to calm down before I rip Micah's spleen out through his belly button.

"Just to be sure," I say as I close my office door, "nobody's hurt? Sick? The village hasn't burned down?"

He glances up from where he's flopped down on the comfortable leather sofa against the far wall. It's my thinking space for when I have big decisions to make, *not* a place to nap. No matter what anyone says.

"Why would you think that?"

Relieved, I join him. "You don't normally turn up here without letting me know you're coming," I point out. "What was I supposed to think?"

"Not that people were dead." He rolls his eyes, then winces. "Although I might wish I was dead after I tell you this."

I still. "What have you done?" My cousins and I have always had a policy of being honest with each other. We routinely fuck with each other's lives, but there's no secret-keeping or slyness about it. Still, normally we're not this dramatic. He's almost acting like a hellhound.

"It's Zac's fault," he declares, throwing him under the bus without hesitation. "If he hadn't been flapping his jaw, I never would have said anything, and Isaac never would have heard anything."

"Isaac?" I think of my adorable little cousin and wonder if Micah and Zac have accidentally corrupted him and now want my help hiding from Grandmother for the rest of their lives. It's not going to happen, of course—I've tempted fate enough times in regard to Grandmother lately. No way will I risk getting on her bad side now that I'm finally on the good one. I'll betray them all in a heart-beat. "What did Isaac hear?"

Micah waves his hand. "He doesn't know what he heard. He misunderstood it anyway. But Garrett..."

I sit up straight. "What about Garrett?"

Sighing, Micah admits, "Isaac repeated stuff at school today and I think Garrett's mad at me."

"Because what he repeated was inappropriate?" I can see why he'd be mad, but he'll get over it. Kids hear inappropriate stuff all the time, no matter how careful you are. Garrett will probably lecture Micah and Zac and give them the cold shoulder for a couple of days, and it'll be fine.

"No. Well, yes. But mostly no." He must see the look of blank incomprehension on my face, because he sighs. "Okay, so at family dinner last week, Zac and I were watching you fawn over Garrett like the pathetic lapdog you've become—"

I raise a brow. "Don't be jealous, Micah. I'm sure one day someone will decide they're lonely and settle for you."

"—and talking about how sad it is that you're so hung up on him," he continues, ignoring me. "Zac might have wondered why you were so obsessed, and then I said I didn't know and maybe he poops glitter."

I stare at him, surprised by the immensity of the anger and betrayal clawing at my chest.

"I'm sorry," he says, looking me straight in the eye. "I haven't been able to talk to Zac yet, but you know he'll be sorry too. We never meant for anyone to hear us, and especially not for Garrett to find out. We like him, Asher, you know—"

I hold up a hand to stop him. "Wait. Just… Let me make sure I've got all this. You and Zac were belittling Garrett and made a stupid joke about glitter and shit, which guaranteed that Isaac was going to repeat what you said *because he's five*, and now Garrett knows about it?"

He takes a breath. "Yes. Though, to be fair, we were belittling you more than Garrett."

I stand and pace three angry strides away, then spin and come back. "You don't think wondering why I'm 'obsessed' with him isn't belittling? As though there aren't a million reasons he's worth any obsession?"

Micah gets to his feet also. "Asher, we were wrong, and it was stupid. I've apologized to Garrett and will again, and I know Zac will too. And yeah, we think Garrett's a great guy. He's kind and good with the kids, he handles Grandmother, and he's already doing good things for our community. But you can't pretend he's the love of your life, Ash. We both know he's not your usual type, not for more than a night, anyway. And we both know that this thing between you isn't love. You guys didn't meet, start dating, and fall for each other. What you've got is a business agreement, and sure, you might be friends now too, but it's not outside the realm of reasonable for me and Zac to wonder why you're suddenly acting like the sun rises in his eyes and sets in his ass."

I clench my teeth so hard, my jaw hurts. His words batter against my brain, but he's wrong. My behavior around and toward Garrett is totally reasonable in our situation.

Isn't it?

Damn him.

"I'm marrying Garrett. He and I are friends, and we sleep together. He's a good man, kind and funny and sexy. I don't appreciate you making snide comments about our relationship." I take a breath and try to let go of my anger. I'm overreacting and I know it, but I hate the idea of Garrett being disrespected. "You and Zac need to apologize to Garrett—profusely—and never, ever again talk about him that way. For your sake, I hope Isaac forgets this quickly and never mentions it to anyone else, because I won't tolerate Garrett being upset any further."

He sighs, still a little mad himself, but since Garrett's been embarrassed at school by this, and those kids might go home and tell their parents all about it, he can't deny that he did the wrong thing. A hundred years ago, we would have beat each other into unconsciousness, but we're mature now. "It won't happen again," he promises. "But you need to think about why it matters so much."

As soon as I hear the outer door close, I go to my desk, sweep up my phone, and punch in Garrett's contact.

"Hey," he answers. "I talked to my mum, and she's excited about helping. She had a bit of a gripe about all the requirements I gave her, but I'm pretty sure she'll come up with the right answer." He chuckles, and the sound goes a little way to relaxing my tense muscles.

"That's good," I reply automatically. "Uh… Micah was just here."

There's a sharp little silence. "You sound mad," he says finally.

"I am. Not with you," I rush to add, just in case he misunderstands, but he chuckles.

"No, I know that."

"Aren't you mad too?" He seems so calm. I expected him to be upset.

"Yes. Explaining to six little kids that I don't shit glitter wasn't something I thought I'd have to do today, and the fact I had to do it because Micah and Zac were being bitchy really annoys me. I'm also hurt. I thought your cousins liked me, but…" He trails off and exhales hard.

"They do like you," I assure him. "And they're both so sorry. They were picking on me, really, but you ended up as collateral damage." I can't believe I'm defending them, but I hate that Garrett is sad about this. "They're both huge morons."

He huffs a laugh. "That, I know. It's fine, Asher. Really.

I'm not upset. Well… maybe a little, but I think it's more ego than anything else. It's not fun to find out people don't think you're worth obsessing over."

"You are. And it's not that… they know you are," I stumble. "They were just surprised because they know how things really are between us and didn't expect me to be so… obsessed." Am I obsessed with Garrett?

Yes.

Is that abnormal? We're getting married. Shouldn't I have a healthy amount of obsession for him?

"I know," he assures me. "It's really fine, Asher. Like I said, mostly ego. Though I wouldn't be against it if you wanted to frown at them for a while."

Nearly all my tension dissipates. I'm still mad at my idiot cousins for their lack of respect, but if Garrett's okay, I'm okay. "Consider it done," I promise, sinking into my desk chair. "Other than Isaac's little revelation, how was the session with the kiddies this morning?" He'd been looking forward to it for days.

His laugh flows down the line and warms me, and I glance at the time on my computer screen. Would it really be so bad if I went home early? Sure, I'd need to blow off a meeting later, but I could spend the rest of the afternoon with Garrett.

"You should have seen them when we played tag," he's saying. "They kept trying to grab my tail, even though it's a small, constantly moving target and the rest of me is so big. And then they worked out they could climb on me, and they lost all interest in tag and just wanted to have a nap on my back."

I snort. "All of them?" I know hellhounds are big, and children are small, but the difference doesn't add up when there are so many kids in the equation.

"When they realized they wouldn't all fit, they started

trying to push each other off. That's when I had to shift back. I think it was a productive lesson, though. Sid said they were talking about what they learned when they went back to the classroom."

"That's great. What are you doing now?" Maybe he'll have some free time, and I can sneak back for a quickie and a snuggle.

"Writing up my observation notes, then meeting the postmaster," he says, and I wave goodbye to my half-baked plans. Garrett is dedicated to his work. I might have been able to convince him if it had been wedding planning, but not work.

"How do you feel about dinner here in Zurich tonight?" I suggest instead. "I don't have to work late. I can come and pick you up—I know you don't love to teleport, but—"

"Yes. Can we go someplace that has fancy cocktails? The bar here is great, but not so much with the mixed drinks."

I grin. He's right about that. The tavern has about fifteen different types of beer on offer, and a decent selection of wine too, but no blender and no fancy mixers.

"Of course we can. Dress up, and I'll find somewhere special." Some time just for us, with nobody else poking their head in or making stupid comments, is just what we need.

CHAPTER THIRTEEN

Garrett

I LOOK around the restaurant Asher's brought me to with a smile. As far as "special" goes, this place is the jackpot. It's even community-owned, so the dining room we've been seated in is exclusive to our people. Asher doesn't have to hide his horns, and the serving sizes are suited to our higher metabolisms. Eating in human restaurants is nice, but I'm always hungry and have to get more food after. They look at us weird if we order as much as we actually need.

Aside from being friendly to our kind, it's posh, with an emphasis on the *osh*. Heavy damask tablecloths, sparkling crystal—in the stemware and the modern chandelier— silverware so shiny it shows my reflection. There's a pianist in the corner providing background music, and the whole vibe is mellow, hushed, and intimate.

I smile across the table at Asher and sip the cocktail I ordered to have with our hors d'oeuvres. "This is perfect."

His answering smile is demon-subtle, but I've gotten excellent at reading his expressions, and I can tell he's pleased. "Good. It occurred to me that you haven't left Hortplatz since you arrived, and I thought you might need a short break."

Oddly, that hadn't occurred to me. One of the first things we discussed with Jesse was arrangements for us to be able to leave the village, and he organized a group of demons who were willing to be called on for teleport duties while we work on a more sustainable long-term plan. Even though the road hasn't closed yet, it's a long, uncomfortable drive to anywhere else, so Annie and Sid have both utilized the "teleport team," as they're calling themselves, a few times already. I, on the other hand, have been so caught up in work and wedding planning and—if I'm being truthful—Asher to even notice that I hadn't left.

"I did," I agree, because the change of scene has definitely had an impact, although I didn't realize I'd needed it. "But living in the village hasn't been as difficult as I thought it would be. Maybe that will change over winter."

His nod is knowing. "Probably. It's always harder when the snow starts. Not so much on the good days, but when there's a weeklong blizzard, it can be hard to enjoy the town."

I've already heard a lot about blizzard season, and the school has an entire binder for procedures during those times, so I'm not surprised by "weeklong." Not thrilled about it, but not surprised. From the sounds of it, the residents of Hortplatz make only minor adjustments to their lives during blizzards. It probably helps that they're all demons and can avoid going outside, instead teleporting from building to building.

Thinking of all the snow I'm going to face over the next six months is daunting, so I change the subject.

"Zac and Micah came to talk to me this afternoon." It's not a happy topic, but I want to get it out of the way.

Seeing the way Asher's face sets confirms that bringing it up was the right thing to do. We need to put this behind us. "I'm convinced that they're both extremely sorry." Zac asked me, in all seriousness, to punch him in the face to even things out. I declined—any idiot knows punching in the face is just asking to dislocate or break fingers, or at the very least end up with a swollen hand—but we did agree that he owes me the favor of my choice, to be redeemed at any time I see fit.

"They damn well should be," Asher grumbles, and I study him.

"Why are you so upset by this? They were stupid and careless, and yes, what they said didn't make me feel great, but they didn't say it to my face. They didn't even say it to other people. We both know neither of them would ever have publicly expressed an opinion that could hurt or embarrass me." I believe that absolutely. Not so much for my sake, though neither is the kind to deliberately hurt someone else, but because they would never do anything to harm their family. I've seen Asher with his cousins, and they're a unit. They fight and pick on each other and occasionally call each other names that can't be repeated in public, but when it comes to the rest of the world, they'll close ranks and defend each other to the last breath.

"And yet, here we are." His voice is cold, but I'm convinced it stems from hurt rather than true anger. "The words never should have been said aloud."

"I agree." I reach across the table and take his hand. His warm fingers wrap around mine immediately. It's nice. "But they were. The guys have apologized, sincerely, and I believe they mean it. Frown at them for a few days, beat them up, and then let it go. Being mad at them is just going to make you miserable."

His expression thaws, and he raises a brow. "Beat them up?"

"They'll probably even let you get a few clean hits in first. Zac offered to let me hit him."

That gets a faint smile. "You shouldn't have said no. I'd pay money to see that."

Chuckling, I let go of his hand and pick up my drink. "How d'you know I didn't say yes?" Perusing the platter of hors d'oeuvres, I select something that looks meaty and take a bite. Mmm… chicken and pancetta, and some sort of cheese. Delicious.

He watches indulgently as I chew, then shakes his head. "You'd never agree to hit someone. If you didn't do it in the heat of the moment, it wouldn't happen. You're too thoughtful."

Aww. That's sweet. I gesture toward the platter. "You can have the next pick."

"I wasn't aware we were taking turns." But he's quick to make his selection. "Tell me about the place where we're getting married."

"Officially, we haven't picked anywhere yet," I warn. My mother hasn't called back yet.

He waves dismissively. "I know, but you're manipulating the situation, aren't you?"

"Of course." He knows me so well already. "My aunt and uncle—Alistair's parents—have a farm in Devon. Well, they call it a farm, and technically I suppose farming does happen there, but it's more like an estate. They live in a lovely late-eighteenth-century manor house with a spacious ballroom and about thirty bedrooms. There are three decent-sized villages within a twenty-minute drive, and Bideford is only half an hour away, so there won't be any trouble finding accommodation for our guests. My cousin Elinor got married there a few years back, which means there's already a list of community-friendly hotels and B&Bs in the area." I smile just thinking about how much easier that will make everything. "We're guaranteed for them to have availability at short notice, since it's a private home, and my aunt has a lot of contacts in the area due to all the entertaining she likes to do." That branch of the family has always been particularly sociable. Which probably explains Alistair.

"It sounds perfect," Asher says. "And the weather should still be quite mild."

I narrow my eyes. "By Hortplatz standards, yes. But November in England is often miserable."

"We can wait until next summer?" He says it as though we're likely to still be together then, instead of "broken up." I don't bother to remind him that I'll be dumping him and going back to Cambridge next summer.

"No, let's get this done. I'm interested to see if actual marriage rather than just engagement has any impact on how the village treats me." I grab another hors d'oeuvre.

"Is someone mistreating you? Being rude?" That edge is back in his voice. Is it wrong that his overprotectiveness gives me warm vibes?

"Not even close. Everyone's been lovely, and even more so since 'us' happened." I gesture between us. "Which is the point. I want to see if they go from being 'friendly and welcoming' to making me one of the cool club members." And I really want to attend the midwinter ritual.

He relaxes. "The cool club? I'm offended that I haven't been asked to join."

"Pfft. You're a founding member." I snitch the last hors d'oeuvre while he's busy pondering that. "They worship you in Hortplatz."

"No." He shakes his head, his gaze tracking the movement of the hors d'oeuvre to my mouth. I take a bite with no remorse at all. "There's no worship. They're just grateful for everything my grandparents have done, and that carries over to me."

I pause with the second bite midway to my lips. Is he really so self-effacing that he believes that? Surely not—the Asher I know isn't lacking in confidence at all. He's aware of his talents and achievements and makes the most of them.

Just as I'm wondering how best to ask, his hand snaps out and steals the food from mine.

"Hey!" I barely manage to keep my voice down enough to avoid attracting attention. "That's mine!"

Asher pops the half hors d'oeuvre into his mouth. "Mmm. Delicious." His head tilts as he smiles at me. "Honestly, Garrett, you should know by now that one thing I'm *excellent* at is reading my opponent."

It's so close to what I was just thinking—that he knows how to make the most of his talents—that a laugh escapes me. Damn him, he *knew* I wouldn't be able to resist an analysis of social behavior. He deliberately distracted me.

"That's how tonight is going to be, hm? We're going to use our special gifts against each other?" I slide my foot out of my shoe and rub my big toe against his ankle, then higher. My sexual weakness for him is just as strong as his for me, but let's face it, that's a battle that will end in a draw, and I'm good with that.

He swallows hard. "Truce?"

Chuckling, I pull my foot back and return it to my shoe. "Truce… for now." I meet his gaze. "We can stay at your apartment tonight, can't we?"

"Yes." His answer comes fast. "I'll take you back in time for school tomorrow."

Our server appears then, whisking away the empty platter and our empty glasses with unobtrusive efficiency.

As soon as he's gone, Asher says, "I've been meaning to mention… I'm pretty sure you know this already, but we're going to need beefy security at the wedding."

I nod. It hadn't occurred to me at first, but when I started thinking about the guest list, there was no way to avoid it. The lucifer is coming, since he's living with Asher's cousin, and then there's Jesse, and Alistair's boyfriend, Aidan, who's my own species leader. With three such high-profile public figures, we can't expect the wedding to slip under the radar for too much longer. I'm convinced the only reason it has for so long is that we don't appear in public and haven't made any concrete plans yet. "Has your cousin said anything about how they want to handle it? Alistair's been shockingly quiet on the subject, which makes me think we should be concerned."

"Concerned?" Asher frowns his scary demon frown, and I'm quite proud of how unaffected I am. But then, he's not really aiming it at me, is he. "Why would that concern you?"

"You'll understand when you know him better. If Alistair is quiet about something, it means his ideas are… over-stated." I wouldn't be surprised if he decided to build a twenty-foot steel-reinforced wall around the estate, then outfitted it with canons and had his sorcerer friends ward the whole thing so strongly that birds couldn't even fly overhead. I don't mention that to Asher, though. There's no point warning him about my family before he meets them.

"Okay." He sounds dubious, but lets it go. "I asked Gideon if there were specific procedures we needed to know about. He said that since three members of the lucifer's team would already be in attendance at the wedding, he trusted me to oversee the rest of the security measures. But I was thinking, maybe we could invite the rest of the senior team as well?"

That's not a bad idea. I tap my forefinger against my lip. "That would work nicely. I met them all at Ellie's wedding, and they were mostly well-behaved."

"Mostly?" Asher's frown is back. "What do you mean?"

"Don't worry about it. The worst ones were already on the guest list." Because they're related to me. The only other one who seemed truly troublesome was— "Oh, wait. That might be a problem."

The sommelier bustles up right then with the wine we ordered to go with dinner, and we go through the process of uncorking and sampling. When everything has been pronounced excellent, our wineglasses have been filled, and we're alone again, Asher looks across the table at me. "Problem?"

It takes me a moment to realize what he means. "Yes. Andrew Turner."

Asher blinks uncomprehendingly twice, and then his eyes widen. "He's in Grandmother's gallery. She's not very fond of him."

"The story I heard was that she tried to kill him."

Our eyes meet. Do we want our wedding to be the site of a rematch? Admittedly, it would be wonderful entertainment. But the bill to clean blood out of my aunt's carpet probably isn't worth it.

"I'll talk to her and see how difficult it would make things," Asher says, wincing slightly. Every time he's talked to her about the wedding lately, it's been to give bad news.

"Tell her how much I loved her idea to use winter foliage instead of flowers for decoration," I offer. I've already told her that, but it can't hurt to mention it again. "You can say I gushed, if you want."

His grateful look is worth any amount of gushing I might have to do, and as our server glides over with our next course, I find myself thinking how much I'm looking forward to observing our wedding guests. Asher's family and mine, plus a few random friends thrown in for contrast.

It's going to be the party to end all parties.

CHAPTER FOURTEEN

Asher

THE DAY HAS COME.

Today I'm marrying Garrett, and I can't seem to stay still. Pacing doesn't really help with nerves. Whoever decided it does was deluded. Yes, it helps to spend nervous energy, but since it does nothing about the cause of the nerves, you're just left walking back and forth in a line like an idiot indefinitely.

Like I am now.

I don't know why I'm so nervous. After all, this is really just the contract signing on another business negotiation… and it's not even one that's been difficult. Garrett and I are both wholly committed to moving forward with this. It suits and benefits us both. All the prenuptial contracts have been agreed on and signed—our legal arrangement is already in play. This is just the icing, a show for our families.

So why am I behaving as though I fear being left at the altar?

Micah and Zac watch me, their eyes tracking back and forth as though they're at a tennis match. Neither of them has said a word about my nerves, which is unusual for us. I know what's holding them back—it's been a month since the drama over their loose lips, and they don't want to risk making me mad again.

Dammit.

"It's fine," I snap. "I forgave you. You were idiots, but that's nothing new. It's over now, Garrett's over it, so it's in the past."

They both stare at me.

"Are you sure?" Zac asks. "Really, really sure?"

"Yes. I've told you that before."

"Thank you." Micah speaks quietly as he stands. "We'll always regret that we made him feel bad, Asher. And made you feel bad."

Aw. My family loves me. "I know."

He nods. "Good."

"What the fuck is wrong with you?" Zac asks. "Are there ants crawling up your legs? You haven't been this fidgety since we were children."

Ahhh, there it is. Something in my chest relaxes. "I'm getting married, you doofus. I'm supposed to be fidgety."

Micah snorts. "He's nervous, Zac. Try to understand. He's finally found an attractive, intelligent person willing to marry him, and he's terrified Garrett will realize Asher's punching above his weight and run away."

Zac smiles slyly. "I bet that's where Gideon is. Garrett's run away, and the lucifer's sent his people to try to find him."

Panic seizes me. I didn't give any real weight to the idea that Garrett might back out, but Gideon *was* supposed to be here an hour ago, and the whole scenario is plausible. What if—

The door to the sitting room we're waiting in opens, and Gideon strides in, frowning fiercely, even for a demon.

"Any luck?" Zac asks brightly.

"No," Gideon replies, and my knees wobble as I gasp.

"Whoa, Asher!" Micah and Zac lunge for me. "Take a breath. Breathe!"

I suck in air. "I'm breathing."

"I was joking," Zac promises. "I swear. I don't know what Gideon's talking about, but I was joking."

"You've always been warped," Gideon says. "What was the joke?"

Micah pushes me into a chair. "That Garrett's run away and the lucifer sent you to find him."

Gideon's scowl gets even blacker. If I wasn't distracted by thoughts of Garrett leaving, even I might be intimidated by it. Though he used to frown like that when he was a toddler, too, and it was so adorable then that the memory of it makes it less scary now. We used to call him our murder baby, because he always looked like he was plotting homicide.

"Garrett's in the room across the hall," he snaps. "Whose stupid idea was it that you had to be apart before the ceremony, anyway? Neither of you are that fussy. Why couldn't you put on your damn suits and wait in the same room?"

I think there might be something more going on here, but I need to be absolutely certain… "Garrett's across the hall?"

"*Yes*. And Sam is also there, because that idiot hellhound you're going to be related to insisted their 'bond as bestest besties' meant Sam was part of *his* family first." He folds his arms across his massive chest. "Have you ever heard anything so stupid in your life?"

I exchange a glance with Micah. "Are you… Are you pissed off because your boyfriend is in another room for" —I glance at my watch—"the next twenty minutes?"

His glower is all the answer I need.

"Here," Zac says, opening my overnight bag and dumping the contents on the bed. "This stuff's a mess. Organize it for us?"

Gideon's no fool; he knows he's being managed. But he also can't resist the lure of a messy pile of crap, especially when he's in a bad mood. It takes less than ten seconds for him to cave and stomp over to the bed.

While he busies himself sorting my belongings into categories, I mull over what he told us. "By 'that idiot hellhound,' did you mean Garrett's cousin Alistair?" I really hope so. There are a lot of hellhounds here right now, and I'll be mad if he's insulted some other member of my future family. Since he already knows Alistair, I'm assuming they insult each other all the time.

"Who else?" he grumbles. "We got here, and next thing I know, Alistair's saying Sam can't come with me to wait with you because he has to go with him to wait with Garrett. Nothing would convince him otherwise, and believe me, we all tried. I should have brought him with us to visit over the summer and let you all deal with him."

Let us… deal with him? "Gideon, I'm not sure if you're aware of this, but I'm an investment banker, Micah is an architect and engineer, and Zac's a geologist and botanist. You're the scary one."

Gideon stops sorting and looks up at me. "He had a T-shirt with a picture of both our faces on it."

"I might have turned violent after seeing that," Zac muses. "At the very least, I would have been annoyed enough to teleport him into the mountains and let him find his own way back."

"Was there a caption?" Micah asks.

"Something about us being bros on world tour,"

Gideon mutters, beginning to fold my shirts with military precision.

Micah pulls a face. "Thanks for not bringing him. I think that would have ruined the visit."

Low-grade panic is starting to build in my gut. This guy is going to be my cousin by marriage in about an hour. What if he wants us to wear matching T-shirts?

"Is there a legal loophole if you kill a family member who's that annoying?" I ask.

"No." The answer comes from all three of them.

"Believe me, that's how Alistair is still alive," Gideon adds. "Sometimes he even annoys other hellhounds. A couple of years back, we had a hellhound mutiny in the office because he said something stupid, and Sam had to threaten to stab him again to make him apologize and fix it."

I smile weakly. Maybe marrying into a hellhound family wasn't the smartest decision I ever made. But… Garrett. He's so perfect. Sure, I might have been able to find someone else willing to enter into a marriage of convenience with me, but it's unlikely we would be as great together as Garrett and I are.

"Wait," Zac interrupts my thoughts. "Did you say 'again'?"

"What?" I ask, but he's staring at Gideon.

"Did you say Sam threatened to stab Alistair *again*?"

I… completely missed that. Sam stabbed someone? Maybe I can see that… if he was mad. He got a little worked up when he was visiting over the summer, and it made me cautious. You know, the way you get cautious when a toddler's running full speed at you and you think there's a chance they might headbutt you in the junk.

"There was this thing not long after we got together with a pencil and Alistair's hand." Gideon's not really paying attention to us anymore, too focused on stacking my now neatly folded clothes.

"Sam stabbed his friend with a pencil?" Micah's almost choking. "That's beautiful."

Is my whole family this warped? Or just the ones in this room?

I think of Grandmother and decide it must be an inherited trait.

Speaking of… "Is Andrew Turner with Garrett too?"

"No, he and the others went to mingle."

Immediately, my imagination throws up visions of Grandmother diving through the wedding cake to stick a makeshift stake in Andrew Turner's heart. "Gideon! Grandmother's out there!"

"Wait, Andrew Turner? From the gallery wall?" Zac asks.

"Yes!" I start toward the door. I don't hear any screaming yet, and that's the only reason I'm not teleporting. I don't want to cause a panic if there's nothing to panic about yet.

"It's fine," Gideon says. "Noah's with Andrew, and I called Grandmother last week and specifically told her she couldn't kill him today. She agreed it would ruin the wedding and promised not to touch him." He puts the last item back in my overnight bag, then turns his attention to us. "Things might get a little tense, but nobody's going to cause trouble with Sam here." There's a heavy threat in his tone. Anyone who *does* cause trouble is going to regret it.

"Who's Noah?" Micah asks. "Wait, you mean Noah Cage, your team admin? The little human? How's he going to stop Andrew Turner from killing our grandmother?"

That's an excellent question.

"Trust me, Noah can be scary. And he has Andrew

wrapped around his little finger." Gideon's distaste is clear, but it seems hypocritical to me, since he's currently sulking over being separated from Sam.

"Plus, the way I heard the story, Grandmother wanted to kill him, and he just kind of rolled with it," Zac says thoughtfully. He's always been the most interested in the gallery, so he'd know, but I'm still a little worried. This wedding can't start soon enough.

With that single thought, my nerves come flooding back, and I get up and start pacing again.

"Why's he doing that?" Gideon asks.

"He's nervous," Micah replies.

"What for? I thought this was a business deal. Business never makes him nervous."

"Some business is more personal."

I happen to turn in time to see Gideon's face at that moment. He looks like he smells something rancid. "Business isn't supposed to be personal. If it's personal, it's not business."

"Since when did you become Mr. Wall Street?" I snap. He's right, damn him. Garrett and I might be doing this with contracts and agreements and an out clause and tentative end date, but I don't think of him as a colleague or associate. He's my friend… who I fuck. But more than that. He's… my partner?

In this agreement.

So… in a way, it's not personal at all.

I shove down the voice in the back of my head that's scoffing and calling me an idiot. It sounds a lot like my late grandfather. He was a loving and affectionate demon, but he had no issue telling things like they were, no matter who he was speaking to.

"I'm just saying, if you're nervous about this arrangement, maybe it's not business. Maybe you're in a relationship and marrying your boyfriend."

There's no air in my lungs, but Gideon doesn't seem to notice that I can't breathe.

"If you can't treat this like a marriage of convenience, if you can't maintain a certain level of detachment, then you should call it all off. Ask Garrett on a date and build your relationship, but don't throw yourself into a marriage headfirst if your expectations are different. That's just asking for it to get messy."

Memories of me and Garrett on what's become our weekly date night flash through my brain. Am I dating my future-husband-of-convenience? Does Garrett know? Is Gideon right… is this all going to become a disaster?

Fuck. Maybe the best thing is just to call this wedding off.

CHAPTER FIFTEEN

Garrett

"Never fear, I've arrived!" The door bangs against the wall as Alistair makes his loud and annoying entrance.

"Yay," I say flatly. It's been barely two minutes since I chased my parents and another of our cousins out of the room. Can't a man have some peace and quiet before he gets married?

"Oh, come on, you know you've been desperate to see me." Alistair bounds across the room and catches me in a tight hug. "It's okay, Garrett. I'm here now."

Somehow, I'd forgotten how much *more* he is in person.

When he finally lets go, I take a moment to straighten my suit jacket, then look past him to the people who followed him in.

"Ellie." I smile, shoving Alistair aside so I can go to our cousin. They work together, but I haven't seen Elinor since her wedding several years ago in this very house. I hug her —a normal hug. "How are you? Where's Javier?"

"He's gone with the others to find seats and be social. I thought David could use another sane person to anchor him."

I don't really understand what she means by that, except that our family is insane. Nobody would deny that.

Turning to the men standing beside her, I hold out my hand. "Thank you for coming."

Aidan takes my hand. "I'm honored to be here." He hesitates. "You know that I know…?"

I nod. "I didn't expect Alistair to keep it secret from you. Or you," I add, glancing at Ellie. I'm fairly certain their whole work team knows this isn't a real marriage.

Well, it's real. It's just not… organic.

"And the whole thing was my dumb idea," Lucifer Sam announces. "So… sorry? And hey, you've been living in the same town with Damaris for three months now and you're still alive. That's a great sign."

I laugh. "She's not that bad. Uh… did Andrew Turner come with you?"

"Yes, but don't worry. He swore to stay away from Damaris. And Gideon called her, and she promised no death at the wedding." He smiles widely, but it seems a little forced to me. "Everything's going to be fine."

The sentence is punctuated by the pop of a champagne cork, and we turn almost as one to see that Alistair has produced a bottle from somewhere, complete with glasses.

"Did you bring that with you?" I ask as he pours.

"Yep! I knew you wouldn't be prepared. You've always been a bit behind the eight ball, Garrett. Not like me. I'm always ready for a party." He shoves a glass into my hand and picks up the next one. I glance into the flute and am instantly mesmerized.

"So pretty," I gasp.

"What the actual fuck?" the lucifer demands beside me, reaching over to take my glass. I pull it back and frown at him.

"I'm sure he's got enough for you. This one's mine."

Lucifer Sam blinks at me. "Now I see the family resemblance. Alistair, what the hell? Is there glitter in that booze?"

"There is. I had to order it special, but I knew Garrett would appreciate it." He passes more glasses around.

I'm in a quandary. On the one hand, this is the kind of thing that people stereotype hellhounds for. It's things like glittery champagne that lead to jokes about us pooping glitter. Which… if I drink this, I actually might. So I should hand it back to Alistair and kindly but sensibly tell him no, there will be no glittery shenanigans at my wedding. I'm a *sensible* hellhound. Down-to-earth.

On the other hand, my sparkly champagne is so fucking pretty and I want to drink it all so my insides will sparkle too.

Fuck it. How often am I likely to get married, after all? I lift the glass to my lips and gulp down the contents.

"Whoa!" Alistair snatches it away from me, but it's too late. I've swallowed it all, and I know it's not possible, but somehow I feel sparkly and glittery now. "Dude, you were supposed to pace yourself. Do you know how much this shit cost me?" There's a certain gleam in his eye—dare I say he looks guilty?

"It tastes expensive," the lucifer says. "I like it." And he tips back his glass and drinks it all.

Alistair stares at him in shocked delight. "What is even happening today? Are all my dreams coming true?"

His boyfriend and Ellie have their heads together, sniffing their glasses and muttering to each other. "Al, is this shifter made?" Aidan asks suspiciously.

Rolling his eyes, Alistair refills my and Sam's glasses with the last of the bottle. "Of course it is. What would be the point of bringing alcohol that wouldn't affect any of us?"

I study the glass and take a sip. "It really is nice. And so pretty."

My cousin nods. "Right? Why can't a drink be glittery? When I told them what I wanted, they understood my vision *instantly*."

"For once, it was a good vision," the lucifer comments, lifting his glass in salute. Alistair stops him before he can drink.

"Go easy," he warns. "It's got a slightly higher alcohol volume than normal. Apparently it was the only way to make the glitter float instead of clumping."

Lucifer Sam studies his glass. "How does that even work?"

"I didn't ask. Those kinds of technical details bore me. I'm more of an ideas hellhound. Other people can handle the execution."

"That's the most self-aware thing you've ever said." I smile at him. "Go, you."

"Fuck you, I'm *very* self-aware. Just ask Aidan. I can predict when I'm going to come right down to the second."

I snort glittery champagne up my nose, and it burns. Oh crap, am I going to *breathe* glitter as well as pooping it now?

While I cough and sputter and accept a handkerchief from Aidan to mop myself up—there's glitter on my suit jacket, but I'm not all that mad about it—Alistair crows with laughter.

"Fuck it," Sam says. "Two-drink limit. I drink this fast now so that anything else Alistair has planned will be soft-focus, and then I can't drink any more." He turns to me. "I don't want to get drunk at your wedding."

"That's very consid—"

"I'd hate to make an idiot of myself in front of Gideon's family."

I close my mouth. I've been living in fairly close proximity to Gideon's—and Asher's—family for three months now, and I have no idea how they'd react to a drunken in-law. I think some of them would be amused… but Damaris? Not sure.

I eye Sam's glass. It would make an interesting side study. They've welcomed me to the family because of my connection to Asher, but would their attitude change if I made a drunken fool of myself at a family event? And not just any family event, but my own wedding?

Before I can decide to steal the glass, Sam lifts it to his lips and empties it in two swallows.

Oh, well. This doesn't mean I can't still conduct the experiment, just that it's delayed. That will give me time to decide if it's actually a good idea.

Alistair is chiding Sam about how he was supposed to *sip* the drink, and how can he enjoy life if he never takes time to savor the moment, and I feel the warm fuzz of two glasses of more-alcoholic-than-usual champagne drunk quickly slip over me. I'm not quite tipsy, but I'm… loose. Or, as Sam puts it, everything is now in soft focus.

It's the perfect way to get married—through a romantic lens.

And speaking of… "Come on, it's time. I'm going to marry Asher now." I set down my glass, brush a hand over my glittery suit, and turn toward the door.

Only to be stopped by Alistair. He meets my gaze, and for once, his is dead serious. "Are you absolutely certain you want to do this? If you are, I'm gonna sit in the front row and clap the loudest when the ceremony's done. But if you have even the tiniest bit of doubt, I have a plan to get you out of here." He pauses. "And I *think* I can keep you safe from the scary grandma too. It depends on how afraid you are of falling off the Tower Bridge into the Thames and then disappearing forever."

"That wouldn't stop Damaris," Sam mutters darkly, and Aidan makes a sound of agreement.

Touched—and wondering if there's a way to ensure he never watches another action movie ever—I pat my cousin on the arm. "Thanks, Alistair, but I'm sure about this. Asher and I have an agreement that suits me well." I lean in closer, the booze loosening my tongue. "And he has a magic cock."

Someone makes a choking sound, but Alistair just grins in delight. "Magic? Excellent. You've needed someone to shoot some magic into you."

That visual is a bit much even for my boozy soft focus, but fortunately, he changes the subject. "Righty-ho! It's time to get Garrett married and stuffed with magic cock!"

CHAPTER SIXTEEN

Asher

GARRETT and I meet in the hallway, and a single glance at his calm, smiling face is all I need to regain my confidence. Maybe I *am* too emotionally invested in this marriage, but I'm just going to go with it. I can deal with the fallout later.

I open my mouth to tell Garrett how handsome he looks but find myself wrapped up in a hug from a stranger. "Cousin!"

What the fuck?

The big hellhound squeezes, making it hard to breathe, but then someone pries him off me. "For fuck's sake, Alistair," Gideon snaps, "you're supposed to welcome him to the family *after* the wedding."

"Pfffft," the giant hellhound who must be Garrett's cousin Alistair says. "There'll be a crowd then. Besides, I never do what I'm supposed to."

I straighten my suit as half the people in the hall with us agree with that statement, then I turn back to Garrett. "You look… Is there glitter on your suit?" Did he tell me he planned to do that? He was very firm on the idea of wearing a plain black suit, because, as he said, they're practical, look good in photos, and can be worn again later. I don't remember anything being said about decorating it with multicolored glitter.

He smiles. "Yes. Isn't it pretty? Alistair's responsible for it… though not directly."

I have so many questions, but now probably isn't the time—and honestly, I'm not convinced I really want to know the answers. "Are you ready to get married?"

"Of course."

The last of my nerves vanish.

"Yeah! It's go time!" Alistair fist-pumps the air, then ushers my cousins, Sam, and whoever the other two people are toward the stairs. "Let's get to our seats so these guys can make a big entrance. I bags the front row!"

"It's probably taken," the woman explains with what sounds like forced patience, but Alistair's not listening. He's slung an arm around Gideon's neck—an arm he's likely to lose any second now—and is loudly saying, "In just a little while, we're going to be cousins!"

"I don't think it works that way," Micah ventures, probably to prevent a homicide at my wedding. "Cousin of your cousin-by-marriage doesn't make him your cousin."

I tune them out as they reach the stairs and start down, focusing my attention on Garrett instead. "This is going to be a great day."

Garrett takes my hand. "You bet it is."

We walk down the stairs and across the grand main hall to the ballroom. The ceremony is being held here, and then while canapés are served in the main hall and formal parlor, the caterers will set up tables for the meal later.

Two of the staff are waiting for us at the very fancy double doors. Garrett gives them a nod, and the doors are pushed open in perfect unison. Did they practice that? It seems like the kind of thing hellhounds would insist on practicing.

There's no time to devote further thought to it, because the music has begun to play inside—Garrett's mother wanted a string quartet, but he talked her down to a single pianist—and our guests are all standing.

The walk down the aisle is... interesting. I keep glancing from one side to the other—on the left, my family and friends, dressed semi-formally, standing quietly, faces somber by hellhound standards but clearly showing how happy for me they are.

On the right... I don't even know how to explain it. For starters, I guess hellhounds consider a dress code to be a loose guideline? Or maybe semi-formal means something different to them. I suppose those ripped jeans I saw *were* bedazzled from hip to hem. And the woman who's wearing what looks like a twenty-year-old cotton beach dress *has* paired it with a one-shoulder feathered cape. Every face sports a wide grin; I get six winks; and people keep calling out congratulations.

I knew hellhounds were quirky, but nobody prepared me for this. Sam was definitely right: we're doing our children—and our adults—a disservice by keeping them so isolated. It would be impossible to believe this if I wasn't witnessing it firsthand.

We reach the front of the room, where the celebrant, Melanie, is waiting. I notice that Alistair managed to get his front-row seat. I don't recognize the man sitting with him—he has long, silvery hair, and his features are... fuck me, is he an elf? Or a dragon? I can't tell the difference between them, but is there a being from another dimension at my wedding? Garrett never told me he knew one!

Melanie clears her throat, and I tear my attention away from the stranger. Garrett needs to be my focus right now.

And it's not hard… he's so handsome in his sparkly suit, and he's going to be my husband.

Melanie begins to speak. We agreed on a simple ceremony, with only a few formal words, short vows, and the declaration of marriage. Community weddings have less hoopla than most human ones anyway, since we don't have religion to make things complicated.

Wrapping up her short speech about the beauty of linking two lives and forming a happy partnership (we specifically told her to keep it low-key and not sappy), Melanie says, "And now I invite you all to witness the vows Asher and Garrett will make to each other."

Garrett and I turn to face each other, but before Melanie can say anything more, there's a ruckus in the front row. Alistair and his silver-haired friend have leaped to their feet, and as we all watch, Alistair shifts into his canid form and begins growling ferociously at the guests. His friend lifts his hands, and magic stirs to life. I'm not sure what kind of spell he's using, but the air in the room is suddenly hard to breathe, static electricity crackling everywhere.

"What the fuck?" Garrett breathes.

"Alistair!" a chorus of voices yell. Three people stand from the first few rows of chairs. One is Sam, one is the man who was with us in the upstairs hallway, and the last is David Carew, who works with Gideon and is the right hand of the lucifer. They converge on the two troublemakers with thundercloud expressions.

"What the actual fuck, Alistair?" Sam demands, then turns to Melanie. "Pardon my language."

She blinks twice. "Uh… of course. Lucifer." She's a sorcerer, and Garrett agonized over whether we should hire her or not. He really liked her and thought she'd be the best choice but was worried she wouldn't be able to cope with a half-hellhound wedding. I didn't fully understand his concerns at the time, but I'm beginning to think he may have been right.

Alistair doesn't stop growling, doesn't even look away from the guests. The hellhound half of the room looks intrigued. Some are taking pictures and video. The demon half of the room looks confused and a tiny bit apprehensive. I'm about 90 percent sure that some of them are ready to teleport out at a moment's notice.

"Caolan, what are you doing?" David Carew asks. His voice is very calm, and somehow that's scary. But I recognize the name Caolan—he's David's boyfriend and was an ambassador for the elves before they migrated. Or something. The details aren't all clear, and when I asked Gideon, he told me it was classified.

Silver-haired Caolan keeps his gaze on the guests but says, "We're making sure nobody objects to this wedding. Alistair wants his cousin to be happy. I'm his bro, so I've got his back."

"This is the *best* wedding I've been to in ages," someone in the audience says.

Garrett sighs, leans against me, and takes my hand. I turn my head to drop a kiss on his hair as I try to work out exactly what that's all supposed to mean.

"You and your bro are both going to regret this," David says. "End the spell."

The elf's alien features set stubbornly. "Nobody gets to ruin Garrett's special day."

"I swear to fucki—" Sam starts, but Melanie interrupts.

"I'm so sorry, I just… um… if I understand right, this can all be easily resolved."

All eyes turn to her.

"Asking if anyone objects is a human thing. We don't

have it in community ceremonies. So… there's no need to worry."

Alistair stops growling.

"Did I know that?" that same audience member asks. "All the weddings I've been to, and do you think I can remember?"

Beside me, Garrett huffs. "That's Aunt Vivienne," he mutters. "Steer clear of her."

Before I can ask why, Caolan turns down the power on his spell. The static still crackles through the air, but it's easier to breathe. "Really?" he asks. "Nobody's going to ruin the wedding?"

"Aside from you?" Sam snarks.

"Nobody's going to ruin the wedding," Melanie announces. "I'll personally deal with anyone who tries. I have a special little bind-and-gag weave that I keep for occasions like this."

Whoa. Garrett and I both stare at her, and she shrugs. "Not my first hellhound wedding."

Caolan sighs with relief, and the oppressive static dissipates as he lowers his hands. "That's so good, thank you. If you need assistance, you can call on me."

"Sit the fuck down," David hisses. "Or you'll be the one needing assistance." Frowning, Caolan makes to sit in his front-row chair, but David grabs his arm. "Oh, no. Sit with me this time so I can keep an eye on you." They make their way back to where David was sitting, muttering to each other. My hearing isn't quite good enough to hear them, but from the way Garrett coughs and shifts his weight, I'm guessing his is. I'll ask him later.

We all look at Alistair, who's still in his canid form, sitting now, giving Sam and the other guy big puppy eyes.

"Shift back, Alistair. You're holding up your cousin's wedding." The toffee-haired man's Irish lilt helps me make the connection—this must be Alistair's boyfriend, the shifter species leader, Aidan Byrne.

Alistair whines pathetically.

"So help me, Alistair, I'll smash one of these chairs and use a broken leg as a shiv if I have to," Sam threatens.

"Alistair, dear," my future mother-in-law says from where she's sitting just feet away. "Do change back. I'm rather keen to get the formalities done so I don't have to worry about Garrett being alone for eternity."

"Why do you all keep saying things like that?" I burst out, then regret it when all eyes turn to me.

That seems to be what it takes, though, because Alistair shifts back to biped form. "We say it because we worried," he informs me. "Garrett's awfully picky, and he tends to get caught up in work and forget about the fact that he's a pack animal and should have people around him." He smiles widely at me. "But he has you now, and an entire village of demons." His face suddenly lights up. "He can be the hellhound lord of demons! He—"

Aidan lunges forward and slaps a hand over his mouth. "So sorry," he says to me and Garrett, then glances to the demon side of the guests. "Sorry," he repeats. "He's very excited about this wedding, but he's going to shut up and sit down and let the ceremony proceed." There's a steely thread to that sentence that makes it sound like a threat, and Alistair's eyes widen, then he nods emphatically. Aidan slowly moves his hand, and Alistair blows Garrett a kiss, then sits in his seat and pulls Aidan down into the one Caolan had been using.

Sam glowers at them for a moment, turns the glower on the rest of the guests, as though daring anyone else to cause trouble, and then nods and returns to his seat.

Melanie clears her throat. "Right. Let's get this done."

CHAPTER SEVENTEEN

Garrett

THIS IS IT. The moment I've been excited about for months.

The demon marriage ritual.

Officially and legally, Asher and I are married. And our ceremony was… well, maybe not lovely, but definitely memorable. I might even let Alistair live, since he was trying to prevent disruption when he disrupted proceedings.

But this ceremony feels so much more special, and not just because it's a millennia-old social ritual I've never been able to witness. There are descriptions of it, of course, written by others, but this type of ritual is private even among demons, so I've never been able to see one.

Most of our guests are already mingling and drinking cocktails, but our parents and Damaris—as head of Asher's family—have joined us in the small parlor my aunt said we could use. If I were a demon, the head of my family would be here too. When Asher told me my parents would be a part of this, I called them to make sure they were aware of how important it was. They're both thrilled to be included and have solemnly promised to treat it with the gravity it deserves.

Damaris holds out a hand to each of us, and Asher and I put ours into hers. She smiles, something I don't see often from her. "Today we invite our ancestors to witness the joining of Asher and Garrett. It gives me so much pleasure to welcome you to our family, Garrett, and to join you with us for all the years past to see."

I'm not sure if it's appropriate for me to thank her, so I nod and smile. She releases our hands, and I mimic Asher as he crosses his arms at the wrists and puts his fists to his collarbones.

"Do you both pledge to guard each other's back from any harm?" Damaris asks.

"We do," we reply.

"Do you both pledge to support and care for each other?"

"We do."

"Do you both pledge loyalty to each other, above and beyond anyone else?"

I meet Asher's gaze and remember how he went toe-to-toe with his cousins, his lifelong best friends, because they said something hurtful.

"We do."

His left arm still pressed to his chest, Asher reaches out to me with his right hand. I take it with mine. His palm is warm, and as our fingers twine together in this ancient, sacred ritual, I can't help but think how good it would be to always be able to hold his hand.

"With the blessing of all our ancestors and the love of your families, your marriage is sanctified. Live long and happily together."

ЛЮ

I squeeze Asher's hand for about the millionth time. He's looking a bit shell-shocked, but that's par for the course since we've been accepting congratulations from my relatives for the last twenty minutes. Honestly, part of me is surprised he didn't back out when Alistair pulled his stunt during the first ceremony.

But he didn't. And we're legally married now.

"…best marital advice you'll ever receive," one of my great-great-uncles is saying, and Asher's face is so visibly strained that I'm glad I didn't hear the rest of it.

"That's very kind of you, Uncle Horace," I say, giving Asher a second to catch his breath. "But we mustn't keep you, or you'll miss out on the hors d'oeuvres."

He slaps me on the shoulder in his usual bonhomie-old-boy manner. "Indeedy yes. You're a good lad, Garrett, even if you are a little reserved. Come find me later when it's time for dancing, and I'll show you how it's done." He ambles off, loudly hailing a cousin, and Asher lets out a quiet sigh of relief.

"What did he say?" I ask. "I wasn't listening."

My brand-new husband groans and closes his eyes for a second. "Don't ask me to repeat it. Please. I… there were dolls… and cheese… I just can't."

Ohhhh. "I've heard that one before." Many times. He likes to give advice, and it's not always pertinent to the situation. I've become immune to the trauma. I pat Asher's arm. "Don't worry, your brain will adapt to protect you."

We seem to be done with my relatives, but the demons are all hanging back still. My guess is that they're waiting to be sure the hellhounds have all moved on and it's safe to approach. Even though most of the adults have been out and about in the world and interacted with other species, they do live mostly with only demons, and they're not used to hellhounds. It just makes me more determined to make Hortplatz a multispecies village.

Before I can work out a way to assure Asher's friends and family that it's safe without making it seem like I think they're cowardly, Sam comes over to us, Gideon half a step behind him.

"Congratulations," Sam says flatly. "Forgive me for not sounding more enthusiastic, but…" He trails off and shakes his head.

"Alistair," I say. It's an explanation, acceptance, and curse all in one word.

"I'm sorry I couldn't stop him. He promised to be on his best behavior, and he's been so excited about this wedding… I just assumed things would go smoothly." He shakes his head, and I laugh.

"Seriously, Lucifer, don't worry about it. That was nothing. It was even kind of sweet. I'm fully expecting at least five of the guests to cause trouble later." I'm keeping an eye on them and hope to head them off, but my cousins are sneaky. I just want to avoid what happened at Aunt Cilla's wedding… nobody wants to hear a dozen hellhounds howling the melody of "Firework" by Katy Perry.

They could at least have picked a classic song.

"Please call me Sam," he says. "We're practically related, thanks to these two." He waves a hand at Asher and Gideon.

"Did you ever imagine this would be our lives?" Asher asks his cousin, whose resting bitch face is the thing legends are made of. Scary legends, but still.

"There aren't enough drugs in the world for that kind of trip."

Sam elbows his boyfriend hard enough that he—Sam—stumbles a step sideways. Gideon doesn't move, seemingly unaffected by the elbow. "Are you okay?"

Before Sam can answer, there's a piercing shriek from across the room. "I'm going to *kill you*! I'm going to rip out your intestines and strangle you with them!"

I'm still trying to process that when Gideon mutters, "Grandmother," and he and Asher start in that direction.

"Oh, please," a voice with a distinctly French accent scoffs into the sudden silence. "As if you could find my intestines."

"That's Andrew," Sam growls. "Why am I surrounded by these people?"

"Does someone have popcorn?" Aunt Vivienne asks. "The entertainment at this wedding has been delightful so far. I can't wait to see what's next."

Serendipitously, the crowd parts just then, giving me and Sam a clear view of the would-be combatants. Damaris's face is contorted with frightening rage—I've never seen her look this way before. She's being held back by her sons, Micah, and Zac, and as we watch, Gideon and Asher join them. It's still a toss-up as to whether she'll break free. Incidentally, her daughter is standing idly by, an expression of mild amusement on her face. It's definitely the women of that family I need to watch out for.

Damaris's ire is aimed at a tall, silver-haired vampire about ten feet from her. One corner of his mouth is quirked in a mocking half smile that makes me want to slap it off his face—and it's not even intended for me. Beside him is Noah, the young human who works with Alistair and the others. His annoyed sneer is aimed at Andrew, not Damaris.

"Grandmother, this is my wedding," I hear Asher say. He's keeping his voice low, but hellhound hearing is extraordinary.

At the same time, Noah hisses at Andrew, "I swear to god, if you don't apologize and stop this scene *right now*, there is nowhere in this world or any other you can hide from my wrath."

Andrew squints at him for a moment. Noah lays a hand on his chest, and a second later, Andrew yelps. "Fine, I'll be good." He lifts his gaze to where Damaris has managed to free one arm, despite the best efforts of her family. "Damaris, I'm sorry. I let the champagne go to my head. Let's call a truce and not disturb the festivities any further."

Damaris glares at him suspiciously for another tense moment, then stops straining to escape and nods tersely. "My grandson's wedding is a joyous occasion."

Her sons and grandsons seem a little unsure that she really means it, as it takes them a few more seconds to actually let go, but once they do, I clap my hands and raise my voice to pull everyone's attention away from the would-be combatants.

"As much as Asher and I appreciate the high emotions and enthusiasm our wedding has caused, if there are any further disruptions, Asher and his cousins will be ripping limbs off the instigators. And then teleporting them to an ice crevasse somewhere they'll never be found." I smile and make eye contact with the people I'm sure have trouble up their sleeves. "Let's enjoy the canapés."

As I half turn toward Sam, my hellhound hearing catches Gideon saying, "How come you got the good hellhound and I'm stuck with Alistair?" It's followed almost immediately by Alistair's howl of protest.

I leave them to it as people begin chatting again, and return to Sam's side. A server has stopped to offer him a glass of champagne from a tray, and as I watch, he takes one in each hand. "Want some?" he asks me, and as I reach for one of his glasses, he adds, "No, sorry, these are mine."

It's not a terrible idea, but I need to stay mostly sober to keep my family in control, so I only take one glass from the tray, and as the server leaves, I ask, "Soft focus not soft enough?"

Sam drains one glass quickly, then sips from the second. "Yeah, no. I know I said I had a two-glass limit and I was done, but between Alistair during the ceremony and Andrew trying to start an interspecies war, I think I'm gonna need to be plastered." He lifts his still half-full glass in salute. "Cheers."

ᔕᔑ

"THE MOST IMPORTANT PART," the leader of the community of species, a man who communes with existential magic and is our representative in all things, says, leaning forward and almost overbalancing. "Oh shit. I think there's an earthquake! The floor just moved." He clutches his boyfriend. "Are you fucking me right now? Did you make the earth move?"

Alistair crows with laughter, and my lips twitch too, though mostly I'm trying not to be shocked that our lucifer is as drunk as a college rugby team after winning a match.

That's right. The *whole* team.

Gideon, who's hovering at Sam's side, puts an arm around him and glares at his slack-jawed cousins. "Nobody will ever speak a word of this," he declares, and the threat is clear.

"Speak of what? Is there a secret?" Sam gasps. "Is there really an earthquake that was caused by Giddie screwing me in the powder room before?"

The sound Micah makes is just as indescribable as his expression. "W-What... A-Are... I-I can't..."

"Did he just call Gideon 'Giddie'?" Asher whispers to me. "I heard that, right? It wasn't a hallucination?"

"That's what I heard," I whisper back, leaning against him. Personally, I don't know how Sam has the nerve, even blind drunk.

"Someone tried to call him that when he was a toddler, and he bit them. Broke skin. They needed three stitches."

Sounds about right to me.

"You screwed in the powder room?" Alistair's asking, seemingly unconcerned about the fact that his "bestest bestie" will probably disappear later tonight, never to be seen again after giving his scary boyfriend a pet name. "That wasn't very considerate of you. What if someone had to use it?"

Sam points at him. "There's, like, a kajillion bathrooms in this house. Last time I was here, I opened the door to what I thought was my bedroom, and KABOOM! Bathroom. It's like the bathrooms move around when you least expect it. They're portable. Or, or… the whole house is like a Transformer, rearranging itself when it needs to."

I don't know enough about the Transformer franchise to know if that makes sense, but somehow I suspect it doesn't. "What was the kaboom for?" I ask Asher.

He shrugs. "How should I know? I haven't seen a kabooming bathroom. It's your aunt's house. You know it better than me."

That's true, and since I've never seen a kabooming bathroom here either, I open my mouth to ask Sam about it. Sadly, at that precise moment, the DJ changes the song.

Sam squeals. "This is ma *jam!*" He ducks away from Gideon, somehow managing to avoid the arm that shoots out to grab him, and skids onto the dance floor. "Let's go, bitches!"

As the rest of us stare in horrified amusement, Alistair

and half of our family race to join him on the dance floor. I don't recognize the song or know the steps, but there's something oddly compelling about it all, and my feet twitch a little.

Suddenly, Sam windmills his arms frantically, shouting, and in the next second, he's flat on his back on the floor. Gideon races over, but Alistair's already helping him to his feet.

"'Sokay! I'm okay! Just had a little slippy-dip. They did an excellent job waxing the floor, Mrs. Alistair's Mom Smythe," he calls to my aunt. She smiles widely and blows him a kiss.

Alistair spins in a full circle. "They are kind of slippery," he says. Sam copies his movement, nearly falling again, only to end up giggling profusely in Gideon's arms.

"Hey, handsome," he breathes. "What's a hot piece of ass like you doing in a this like place?"

"This is the best thing I've ever seen in my life," Asher murmurs as hot color burns on Gideon's cheekbones. "I don't want to say it's the best part of our wedding day, but—"

"Oh no, it definitely is," I agree. "Did Sam just stick his hand down your cousin's pants?"

As Gideon struggles to extricate himself from the suddenly octopus-armed lucifer, Damaris appears beside us.

"I'd like to apologize for my outburst earlier," she says stiffly, not looking at either of us.

"No apology needed," I say as fast as I can. "It was Andrew's fault. I have no doubt." There's no way I want Damaris thinking I'm mad at her and might need to be taken out.

"Sure," Asher agrees, still watching Sam trying to unbutton Gideon's shirt in the middle of the dance floor while most of my family cheers him on. "Nobody blames you, Grandmother."

"Thank you." She still sounds very formal, but I think a little less displeased. "It's been a…" She appears to be searching for the right word. "…lovely wedding. The food was excellent, and this house is beautiful," she adds.

"Have you had a tour?" I ask, dragging my gaze away from Sam, who has given up on trying to strip Gideon and now is spinning around him like he's a pole and Sam's a stripper. "I'm sure my aunt would love to show you around."

Damaris's face relaxes. "That's very kind. I was going to speak with her anyway, so I may ask. You two enjoy your night. Who knows how long you'll have, just the two of you." She disappears while that comment is still sinking in.

"Did your grandmother just hint that we should start planning to have kids?" I ask Asher.

"Yep."

Great. Oh, well… it shouldn't be too hard to put her off for seven months until we "break up."

I put a hand to my suddenly churning stomach. Maybe one of those canapés disagreed with me.

Suddenly, the music stops, and I spin around to see Alistair taking a microphone from the DJ. "Oh no," I mutter.

"Hey, folks!" He beams at everyone, and half the room —the half related to me—calls back, "Hey, Alistair!"

"Don't worry, the music will be back in a sec. There's a lot of partying left to do tonight! But I wanted to take a moment to welcome Asher and his family to ours. Hellhounds and demons, united at last!"

Cheers break out—again, from my family. Most of Asher's just look confused.

"Some of you know that Garrett is the most sensible

hellhound alive. He's the one we send when we want people to think we're responsible." Far too many people call out agreement, and I wonder if it's too late to disown my family. "But every hellhound needs some flash and dazzle in his life, so allow me to share with you… my wedding present to the grooms!"

That seems to be a cue, because there's a bang, and suddenly, big pieces of glitter are showering over the dance floor. Another bang, and another shower.

"What the fuck?" Asher swipes the metallic thumbnail-sized plastic away from his face. I sigh and point at the "gift" I've just spotted.

"Glitter cannon," I explain. This is actually pretty low-key as far as Alistair goes. "Thanks, Al," I call.

"It's yours to keep! To add sparkle to your marriage."

Before I can think of a reply, Sam lets out another of those uncharacteristic squeals. "It's like a Slip 'n Slide!"

I watch with dropped jaw as the lucifer skids on his knees from one side of the dance floor to the other, made easy by the slippery pieces of plastic.

Slowly, I raise my gaze to Asher's. I'm not sure what he sees there, but his face becomes guarded.

"What?" he asks warily.

"Come and measure how far I can get."

CHAPTER EIGHTEEN

Asher

THE FIRST TRUE blizzard of the season blows through in early December, just a few weeks after the wedding, and Garrett's not prepared for it. He's never lived anywhere that experiences truly snowy winters, and after the initial fascination passes, he sees the storm for what it is: a pain in the ass.

It's even more of a pain for him than for the rest of us. We're so used to teleporting from indoor space to indoor space that no real infrastructure exists in the village to clear snow from the roads. Some families clear parts of their yards, especially if they have pets that need to go out or children who play outside, and if it gets too high around buildings and becomes a hazard, we deal with that, but otherwise we mostly just wait for it all to melt come spring. That's not an option for our new non-demon residents, who, we discover, are basically trapped in the house. No one in the village considered that because we're not used to having non-demons here, and Garrett and his team didn't consider it because they're not used to this volume of snow.

Which is why I'm sitting on my couch beside my cousins, and we're all being chastised like children by my ranting husband.

He's adorable when he gets all worked up.

"…cannot expect people to rely on someone else every single time they need to leave their home," he's repeating for the third—maybe fourth—time. He's really riled up about this. "When storms end, the streets need to be cleared. You'll never keep other species here otherwise."

Micah side-eyes me, then clears his throat. "You're right," he says, "but, uh… you know we're not in charge of the village, right? Do Zac and I have to be here for this?"

Garrett's eyes blaze, and for just a moment, I pity Micah.

"Yes, you have to be here! I've asked Jesse to call an emergency meeting of the village council for this afternoon so this can be resolved as soon as possible."

"But," Zac ventures, drumming his fingers nervously against his knee, "we're not on the village council."

"Your grandmother is."

It takes only a split second for his meaning to sink in, and then my cousins scramble to their feet. "Oh, no," Zac says. "No. Isn't it enough that we held her back at the wedding? She could have turned on us at any time. We risked life and limb, and she still hasn't forgiven us for interfering."

That's true. Family dinners have been distinctly chilly lately.

"Don't exaggerate," Garrett dismisses. "If she'd wanted to turn on you, she would have, and none of us would have been able to save you." He's remarkably calm about it all, but then, it's not him who would have been ripped apart. "Besides, I'm not concerned that they'll disagree with the need for street crews. It's the urgency that might be an issue."

I keep my mouth firmly shut. Being married agrees with me—I get a friend to talk to, snuggles on a cold winter night, and sex pretty much on tap. There's no way I'm doing anything to upset that if I don't have to. My cousins can fight this battle—and lose.

"I'm not following," Micah says slowly. He knows it's a trap, but he can't resist it. Curiosity has always been his weakness.

"Unlike most of my other suggestions, this can't wait. It needs to be implemented immediately because Sid and Annie and I are living here *right now* and are trapped in our homes *right now*."

That stirs me to protest. "Hey!"

Garrett shoots me a glance. "Yes, yes, you've been my personal teleporter, and you've been teleporting them as well, but that's the entire point. We're completely dependent on you to go anywhere. Work. The store. The pub. The post office. The end of the freaking garden path… not that we could even stand there, since it's buried in four feet of snow right now." The disgust in his tone makes me hide a grin. If he's this unimpressed by the little storm we just had, the big ones that are coming later in the season will infuriate him.

But I do understand where he's coming from.

"So you want Micah, Zac, and me to tell the council how difficult it's been for you and your team?"

"No." He heaves a giant sigh and plants himself on my lap. "We can do that. I need you to tell them how annoying it is to have to teleport us at our convenience. And then I need you to convince them to allocate the budget to get a snowplow up here within the next few days and hire and train someone to use it."

"Done," I assure him. "We can handle that." I put my arms around him and ignore the glares I'm getting from my cousins. We *can* handle that, even if it turns out I have to pay for it myself. "Is a snowplow the only option, though? Sid's a sorcerer—can't he use sorcery to move the snow?" It would be easier than getting a plow up here at this time of year. We're probably going to need to teleport it in, and that's going to take at least four demons working in tandem. Heavy machinery is *heavy*.

"Sid has a job, and it doesn't involve snow removal," Garrett reminds me. "Besides, his sorcery doesn't work that way. Maybe when the village starts actively recruiting other species, they can look for a sorcerer who can do that."

"Wait, you mean there are different types of sorcery?" Zac asks.

We all slowly turn to stare at him.

"What? How was I expected to know that?" His tone is defensive.

"We knew," Micah points out, gesturing between himself, me, and Garrett. "You lived in Paris for fifty years. How did you not know that?"

"I didn't go around asking every sorcerer I saw what their skills were!"

Micah opens his mouth to continue the argument, but Garrett squirms off my lap—dammit—and holds up his hands. "We have more important things to focus on right now. Though… Zac, later we're going to talk. Maybe I should be running adult education too. But now, I need to know I can depend on you all."

"To talk up the plow cause at the meeting? We said we would," Micah assures him.

"No. Well, yes," he corrects. "But I also need your support for Christmas."

That gets him blank stares from all of us. "For what?" I ask.

"Christmas," he repeats patiently. "It's a human tradition."

The pieces click together. "You mean that thing some of them do this time of year with the big trees?" There are several of them in Zurich, along with special markets. I usually ignore it all. I'm in the city to work, after all, and human traditions have never been important to me.

"Yes. I think it's important for the children to be aware of other species' customs. Since we're in Switzerland, it's most likely that when they leave Hortplatz, they'll be going somewhere in Europe, and Christmas is widely celebrated in Europe. On top of that, most of what we teach them about humans is negative, because it's so important that they know to always be wary of keeping our secret. They should know that humans aren't all evil."

"Aren't they, though?" Zac asks. "If you get online and check the human news, it's mostly wars, conflicts, people physically harming each other, people saying harmful things about other humans…"

Garrett winces. "They don't always show their best side. But some… *many* humans are just like us. And the kids need to learn how to interact with them without causing suspicion, so learning some of their traditions is a good step."

Slightly worried that he's thinking of a village-wide festival that I'll have to participate in, I say, "Just to be clear, you want to teach this Chriss-thingy in school? To the kids?"

He laughs and rolls his eyes. "Yes, Ash. I'm not going to make you celebrate a human holiday." He knows me so well already. "But I'm about 90 percent sure the village council will object, so I need your support."

"You've got mine," I say immediately, and stare at Micah until he agrees.

"I don't know," Zac begins, and I wonder if I can teleport to him, pinch him, and get back to my seat without Garrett noticing. Fortunately, Micah handles it for me. "Ow! I mean… sure. Teach our children the customs of a genocidal species that tried to destroy us."

Garrett smiles at him. "Trust me on this, Zac. It's necessary and will make things easier for them when they leave here."

Zac still doesn't look convinced, but he doesn't argue.

"You both can go," Garrett adds. "Just don't forget to turn up to the meeting this afternoon."

My cousins exchange glances. "Uh… we live here?" Zac ventures.

"I know, but since I'm a lot less stressed now, I was planning to strip Asher and ride him like a—"

"Annnnd we're going! Bye!" Zac teleports out without waiting for a reply. Micah's only a moment behind him but laughing so hard, I hope he actually makes it to wherever he's going.

"Ride me, huh?" I lean back against the sofa and extend a hand to Garrett. "Let's talk some more about that."

He grins and straddles my lap. "I was actually thinking a demonstration might be more effective. Since we have the place to—"

"I'm not looking!"

We both look up, startled, as Zac teleports back into the room. He's got his hand firmly over his eyes. "I just wanted to remind you that this is a shared space! We all use that sofa, so please have your married-people sex in your bedroom." Before we can reply, he teleports back out.

Garrett's laugh vibrates through me. "Married-people

sex? Does that mean if we weren't married, he wouldn't care if we fucked on the sofa?"

"I'm pretty sure he's fucked on this sofa," I admit, then adjust his weight in my lap, wrap my arms around him, and stand.

"Ooooh. Impressive. Big, strong demon." Garrett's still laughing, but that doesn't take away from my pride in that feat.

"I'll show you impressive," I promise, heading toward our bedroom. We've been alternating between my room here and his at the house he shares with his team. The official story is that we'll have our own house built come spring, but unofficially, we haven't decided yet if that's going to happen.

But one thing I'm sure about is that we're dynamite in bed.

I drop him on the mattress, and he bounces, then instantly whips off his shirt. "I changed my mind."

Freezing midstep, I say, "What?" Changed his mind?

"I don't want to ride you. I want to lie back and be treated like a prince."

Snorting, I make an elaborate bow. "Of course, Your most Royal Highness."

He sniffs theatrically. "And then I want to be fucked through the mattress."

I bite back a laugh. "I live only to serve, Your Highness."

"Hop to it, then," he demands, but he's grinning. "Serve faster."

I throw my shirt at him and get started on my pants. He wiggles out of his clothes, and when I go to close the bedroom door—just in case—he grabs the lube from the nightstand.

"Give me that, Your Highness. All part of the service."
I join him on the bed and take the tube.

"Hmm, I could get to like this." Garrett snuggles back
into the pillows, bending his knees and opening his legs.
With his cock rapidly hardening and the dark shadow of
his pucker, it makes for a tempting view.

I grab his hips and drag him down a little, adjusting the
angle so I'll have full access, and he mock gasps. "How forceful
you are!" He flutters his lashes at me. "I may just swoon."

"You go ahead and swoon if you need to," I offer,
patting his knee. "I'll just fuck you through the mattress in
the meantime." I lean down and kiss his abdomen, right
along his happy trail under his belly button.

"So dedicated," he murmurs. "Are you sure you can
handle the hardship?"

Shrugging, I squirt lube onto my fingers. "Some sacri-
fices need to be made." I trace my index finger around his
rim, and the muscle there instinctively tightens before he
forces it to relax. "There you go," I croon. "Let me in."

It doesn't take long for me to stretch him, and because
I go out of my way to tag his prostate a few times, he's
soon writhing on the bed and demanding more. I take a
moment to lay a line of kisses along his dick, and he grabs
my ears and pulls my head up. "In me. Now."

"You're so demanding, Your Highness."

"Ash…" It's half warning, half sob, and I free myself
from his grip and line my cock up with his entrance.

We both moan as I breach the ring of muscle. We've
been having so much sex, but every time feels like the first
time… only better, because I *know* him. Know what he
likes, how he'll react. As I sink into his body, I know that
he's going to wrap a leg around my hips. Know that if I
shift my weight just like so… A tremor overtakes him.

I could spend the rest of my life doing this with him and never get bored.

But he asked to be fucked through the mattress, so the least I can do is deliver. Patting his thigh, I brace myself on my knees, then take hold of his hips and go to town. The sound my first thrust wrings from him vibrates through my whole body. *Hold on, hold on,* I warn myself. I want him to come first, simply for the pure pleasure of his ass clamping down around me.

"Asher," he slurs, opening his eyes. They're hazed with lust. "Ash."

I adjust my position, taking things up a notch, and as my cock grazes his sweet spot, he cries out and shudders. A few more thrusts like that bring us both so close to the edge, but I'm not ready for this to be over.

I stop, deep inside him, and lean up his body to kiss him. The movement feels amazing to us both, but with no additional friction, we have time for a breather.

"You're incredible," he whispers against my mouth, and my heartbeat picks up. There's something about being with him like this, locked together in the most intimate way but not striving for orgasm, that makes me feel… whole.

"I live to serve you," I whisper back, and even though it's supposed to be a joke, in this moment, it's not. I kiss him deeply as a distraction.

When we break apart, breathing deeply, he shifts his hips, reawakening all the sensations that just calmed down. I chuckle.

"I can take a hint. So… think I can make you come hands-free?" We've done that once before, but it took a lot of time and effort.

He shrugs. "Consider it part of your service." His hand comes up to cup my cheek. "I believe in you."

I pull back, hope stirring deep inside. Maybe Garrett's

starting to come around to the idea of staying married to me. If sex is what it takes to convince him, that's definitely a sacrifice I can make.

Without saying another word, I get back to work, setting up a fast, hard rhythm, making sure to hit all his sensitive spots. I lay one hand on his stomach, palm down, and feel the muscles react to my touch. Garrett loves to be petted, stroked, and I do that now even as I fuck him so hard that he raises his arms to brace himself against the headboard.

"I wish you could feel you like I do," I pant. "There's nothing in this world that feels as good as you—surrounding me, under me, your skin against mine."

His gaze meets mine, and it seems like he's going to say something, but then his eyes roll back and his whole body seizes up in orgasm. That's all it takes to send me over the edge, and as I fall through eternity wrapped up in him, I send out a silent wish for this to never end.

CHAPTER NINETEEN

Garrett

I FUCKING HATE SNOW. This is something I've just learned about myself. If you'd asked me a month ago, I would have said snow is lovely. I've always thought it charming when it snowed, and I definitely love skiing and have visited various ski resorts across Europe dozens of times over the centuries. There's nothing like a bracing afternoon of snow sports, followed by an evening of more adult sports in front of a roaring fire while the snow falls outside. Ten out of ten, the perfect way to spend a winter weekend.

This snow, however… well, right now I can't think of anything I hate more than this snow. This stupid, constantly there even when it's not snowing, mocking me snow. And the worst part is that I was told about this. I was fully informed. They said the road would be closed because of the snow. They said it sometimes snowed for nine months of the year. Even after I got here and the snow began ridiculously early in autumn, I still didn't realize what that would mean for me. I suppose in my head, I was picturing some kind of movie scenario, where the storm would rage through, cutting off the road and keeping us inside for a day, but when it ended, the village would miraculously still be snow-free. Or just have neat little snowbanks in out-of-the-way places, plus a light ground covering, enough for the kids to make snow angels but not enough to require snowshoes or anything like that. Snowshoes! Blech.

The reality is vastly different. The first real storm, which everyone told me was "a baby storm," deposited feet of snow—right up to the window ledges. And the lack of snow-removal infrastructure in the village meant that even after the sky cleared and the sun came out, the only way I could leave the house was if Asher or one of the others took me.

The second storm of the season deposited enough snow to cover the windows, but thankfully, my emergency pleas to the village council had already resulted in a snow-plow *and*, through some miracle Asher pulled off, a sorcerer who was excited about the challenge of a snowed-in village. Her name is Zoe, and she's the first (hopefully) permanent non-demon resident. Her arrival was completely unplanned, but in the week she's been here, she's proven enthusiastic, helpful, and keen to make the village a multispecies-friendly place. She's gotten a warm welcome, and not just from me. Her idea to not just clear the snow from certain areas, but use it to create more community activity spaces, has been a big hit. For example, the stream that runs near the village, while completely frozen over, isn't really great for skating. Zoe has used the excess snow to create a three-inch-thick sheet of ice for a skating rink on the village green. She's also building a "snow village" outside the village proper, one little house at a time, and the children adore it.

But even with Zoe and the plow working together to

keep roads clear, there's no escaping the snow. It's everywhere.

Muttering to myself as I trudge through it to the school, I resolve to have Asher take me to Hawaii or the Caribbean for a weekend soon. I need to defrost, and the benefit of being married to a demon is that we never have to worry about airfare.

There are other benefits too, and remembering how he woke me this morning is enough to make me smile behind the scarf wrapped around the lower half of my face. I have a sneaking suspicion that I'm getting too attached to Asher, but I've been ignoring all the warning signs. It's only been a few months since we met. Maybe by the time my end date here rolls around, we'll be sick of each other. Until then, I'm just going to enjoy being petted and spoiled and screwed until I scream every night.

I unlock the school, turn up the thermostat, and start turning on lights. I'm the first one here today because I wanted to get a head start on some planning before the kids get here and Sid and Annie might need me. Tomorrow we start teaching the kids about Christmas— and wow, getting permission for that was a huge achievement.

The hours pass as I put together a collection of different Christmas traditions to talk about, then research craft activities. There's a mid-size fir tree at the edge of the playground that we can decorate, but I'd love for the kids to make their own decorations. They won't last very long out in the elements, but it's not like we actually plan to *cele- brate* Christmas.

Annie stops in to bring me tea. "You're my favorite," I tell her, wrapping my hands around the mug and breathing in the fragrant aroma.

"You say that to everyone who brings you tea," she

retorts, smiling. "The kids have started arriving, so it's going to get noisier."

"No problem." One thing about studying people: you get used to working with noise. I've perfected the art of tuning things out.

Proof of that is that I have no idea how much time has passed when Sid knocks on the door and sticks his head in. "Do you have a few minutes?"

I push back from my desk and stretch. "Sure. Did you need me in the classroom?"

He shakes his head and pushes the door open to reveal Isaac with big, wet, woebegone eyes and a trembling lip. "Isaac and Susannah were jostling each other, and Isaac fell off his chair and hit his head."

I'm up and around the desk faster than I would have thought possible. Isaac's already throwing himself into my arms before I can crouch all the way down. "Is he…?" I assume Sid's already done a concussion check. He has minor healing sorcery ability, enough to deal with scrapes and bruises.

"He's fine. A bit shaken, and he says he has a headache. I was going to call his parents to collect him, but he said he wanted a hug from his cousin Garrett."

Aww. Isaac's been getting attached to me lately—which I put down to my awesome storytelling ability—and I can't say it makes me mad. He's a cute tyke. His arms are still wrapped tightly around my neck, face buried against my shoulder, and I really hope the dampness I feel is tears and not snot.

"I'll take care of it," I tell Sid. He can sit with me for a little while, and then I'll either take him home or call his parents myself.

Sid goes back to the classroom, and I stand, lifting Isaac into my arms, and go back to my desk chair. It takes some coaxing to get him to loosen his grip, but finally he's settled on my lap, leaning the side of his head against my chest. I look down at his little tearstained face. "Do you want some water?"

He lifts those big eyes to me. "Juice?" There's a pitiful waver in his voice that tugs at my heartstrings.

"Sure, I've got juice." We keep some in case of low blood sugar incidents. "But I need to get up to get it for you."

Sniffling, he slides off my lap and waits. I hide a smile as I fetch him a juice box, and he immediately climbs back into my lap.

"Better?" I ask as he slurps through the straw.

He nods slightly. "Tell me a story? Please?" The big eyes are aimed at me again, and I don't even bother to resist.

"Sure. Let's see… have I told you the one about the dragon who lives in a cave?" I'm sure I haven't, since I totally just pulled that from my ass. The benefit of discovering that dragons actually exist is that any story I make up with a dragon in it has instant credibility with children. The downside is that I have to be more careful about my descriptions of dragons and their abilities… especially here in Hortplatz, where the kids have no basis for comparison. The last thing I need is for them to meet a dragon one day and grievously offend them because of something I once said.

Isaac thinks about it carefully, his nose wrinkling. "You told me about the dragon who lived at the beach."

I shake my head solemnly. "No, this is another dragon —one who lives in a cave high up in mountains covered in snow."

"Like where we live?" I've piqued his interest.

"You don't live in a cave! I've seen your bedroom. Definitely not a cave."

That gets a giggle. "Nooooo, but we live high up in snowy mountains! And there's lots of caves near here. Micah showed me some last summer."

"That's true," I agree. "Now, this dragon, whose name I can't remember, so we'll call him…" I wait. This is something I do with every story, letting the kids—or kid, in this case—name the protagonist.

"Ed!" Isaac declares. "Ed the dragon."

"Sure. Ed the dragon, it is. Well, Ed was a biiiiig green dragon who lived in an *amazing* cave. It was big enough to hold him in his dragon form with his wings stretched out." I spread my arms as wide as I can to demonstrate. "The cave was very comfortable, even though it was all rocky. It kept the snow and wind out, and the inside was nice and warm."

"Did it have a bathroom?"

I bite my lip to keep from laughing. Of course Asher's cousin would be a practical five-year-old. "Not a bathroom like you or I use, but a special bathroom that Ed could work with his dragon magic."

Isaac nods as if that makes perfect sense. "What did Ed's biped form look like?"

Uhh… "He was not as tall as me," I begin. Height can be tricky for kids—I can't just say "six feet" because they rarely have context for that. And since demons are all, as a rule, tall, Sid and Annie have found that some of the kids expect all adults to be like that. They were both asked if they would continue to grow as they got older.

"Was he as tall as me?"

I chuckle. "He was one and a half of you," I say. "One whole you, and then an extra set of your legs." That method of description delights Isaac, and he puts down his unfinished juice to pay better attention as I weave the story of Ed the dragon, who lived in his awesome cave with his hoard of videogames and books, but got lonely sometimes and eventually made friends with Billy the snow leopard.

"I've never seen a snow leopard," Isaac informs me when I've finished, his voice heavy with doubt.

"No, you wouldn't have. They live in Asia." The teacher in me is tempted to ask if he knows where Asia is, and then pull out a map to show him.

He nods sagely. "He must be traveling, then."

"Something like that," I agree.

"I'm very tired now."

"Let me call your parents," I say, reaching for my phone while studying his face. His gaze is still focused, and he seems to be completely cogent. The tiredness is probably from the excitement.

"I could nap here with you," he suggests. "You could shift, and we could curl up like puppies!"

I still have a lot of work to do, but I can't deny that a nap sounds nice. "What an excellent idea."

Isaac scrambles off my lap and heads toward the sofa along the wall. It's there because this office doubles as a sickbay of sorts while kids are waiting to be picked up. He stops beside it and looks at me expectantly.

I shift, give myself a shake, and bound over the desk, making him squeal in excitement. He waits for me to settle on the sofa and then climbs up. It's a bit snug, since animals my size weren't the designer's priority, but he sprawls half over me, half against the cushions, and we settle in.

Isaac's breathing evens out quickly, and I'm just starting to drift off myself when the office door opens again. I open one eye and peer up at Sid and Chloe.

"Chloe wanted to make sure Isaac was okay," Sid says softly, grinning. "Nobody told us it was naptime."

"I want a nap," Chloe adds wistfully, and Sid raises a brow at me. I whine in assent. It won't hurt her to miss an hour of class, and I know my in-laws won't mind. They've said more than once that they hope Chloe and Isaac will grow up to be as close as Asher, Micah, Zac, and Gideon are. That kind of bonding starts here.

"Go on, then," Sid tells her, and her face lights up. He waits until she's climbed up and found a spot on the now very cramped sofa, then closes the door quietly behind him.

Chloe sighs and rests her head on my haunch, her fingers idly ruffling my fur. "This is nice."

I huff and close my eyes. It really is.

CHAPTER TWENTY

Asher

I'M IN TROUBLE, and I can't deny it anymore. Trouble with a capital T. In fact, all the letters are capitals. And italicized, and underlined. _TROUBLE._

I've fallen in love with my husband.

The same husband who thinks of our marriage as a means to conduct an anthropological study. Who still plans to walk away in six months. Who considers me a friend and fun to fuck, but not more.

Sure, he's fond of me. He likes me. He probably even plans to stay in touch. But I'm so much in love with him, the thought of being apart tears at my being. I'm dreaming of a future together, where we spend centuries, maybe even a millennium, loving each other. We build a home and life together, maybe even raise children together. And he's not thinking any of those things.

I'm so screwed.

"I'm so screwed," I repeat aloud, my head in my hands.

"Yeah," Gideon agrees, and I lift my head to glare at him.

"That's not helpful." I teleported to his house so I could share my problems and hopefully get some advice from a man who's been in a relationship for a long time. So far, that hasn't happened. Although he has been working steadily on his LEGO, which means he's thinking.

I look around the LEGO room. It's the most boring-looking room in existence. The walls are lined with cabinets, inside of which are boxed LEGO sets. Gideon doesn't care about displaying what he builds, so as soon as it's done, he takes it apart again, puts the pieces in carefully labeled Ziploc bags, and then tucks the box away. The cabinets are arranged by series/theme, and then alphabetically. The only other furniture in the room is a large table and a couple of chairs.

"You're sure he doesn't love you back?" Gideon asks almost absently as he builds… something. I look at the box to see what he's making. The title declares "Holiday Main Street." Whatever that is.

"I'm pretty sure he loves me, but not that way." What a dismal thought.

"Maybe he needs time. You haven't known each other that long. I knew Sam for five years before we fell in love."

There's a strangled shout from the hall, and Gideon leaps to his feet. The door bursts open, banging against the wall. "Don't listen to him, Asher!"

Gideon sits back down as I blink. "Uh… okay? Why?"

Sam storms in, glaring at his boyfriend. "We had a one-night stand, then he spent five years alternately ignoring me and making me think he was plotting the best way to get rid of my body. *Then* he started acting all possessive and affectionate, and boom, we were together. Do *not* do any of that with Garrett."

I slowly turn my head to look at Gideon. He doesn't

meet my gaze. "You left a lot of things out when we asked how you and Sam met."

He shrugs. "Details."

Sam's choked scream would be funny if I wasn't worried about losing Garrett forever. "Do you have any advice?" I ask him. "Since you've clearly been eavesdropping."

"It's my house," he reminds me, as though that's any excuse. "And yes, I have advice. Gideon wasn't completely wrong—give Garrett some time. He's already very attached to you, and since you're playacting that you're in love, it gives you a huge advantage. You can show him your feelings without putting any pressure on him."

"Huh?" Dammit, things were so much easier when I just had casual sex.

Sam rolls his eyes. "Be affectionate. Do all the things you want to do."

Yeah, that's not helpful. "Liiiiike…?"

"Are all demons like this, or just your family?" he huffs. "Like… hold his hand in public. Kiss him. Snuggle after sex. Take him out for dinner."

Oh. "We already do all that."

Gideon's head comes up. "You do?"

I shrug. "Sure. Why?"

"That doesn't sound very marriage of convenienc-y to me. Do you cuddle on the couch together too?"

"Sometimes. He's been watching this show that he can't watch when he's alone. So I watch it with him, and we cuddle."

"Do you like the show?" Sam asks, studying me intently.

"I see where you're going with this, and you're wrong."

"Am I, though?" Sam's smirk is thoroughly annoying.

"Yes, I watch the show because I love him—even

though I hadn't realized that—but he doesn't cuddle because he loves me." And ouch, that hurts to say.

"All I'm saying is that this sounds a lot like a real marriage. Giving Garrett time to come to terms with that might be all you need to do." He pauses. "How *did* you realize you love him?"

I sigh, the memory making me feel warm and fuzzy inside. "I came home early from Zurich one day last week and went to the school to surprise him. I thought I could talk him into leaving early and maybe going skating with me while we could have the place to ourselves."

"Because that's totally what people who are only together for convenience do," Gideon mutters.

Ignoring him, I continue, "When I got there, he was curled up on his couch in canid form, asleep with Chloe and Isaac. And I…" I trail off, not having words for how the picture had affected me. "I knew then."

Gideon frowns. "Why were Chloe and Isaac sleeping at school?"

"That's all you have to say right now?" Sam demands. "There is no romance in your soul." He turns to me. "But yeah. Why were they?"

"Apparently Isaac hit his head and wanted to stay with Garrett. He's fine," I assure them. "He just decided a nap was needed."

"Smart kid." Sam looks me directly in the eye. "I only know what you've told us, and some observations from the wedding, but if I were you, I'd just enjoy the next few months. Garrett's really attached to you already. Worst-case scenario, when the time is up and he leaves, you suggest dating long-distance for a while. I don't think he's going to want to end it completely."

"Yeah, but—"

"No, Asher, listen to me. I don't think it's going to

end." He's using this weirdly intent voice and staring at me.

"I appreciate that, but you can't know——"

"Ash, he's saying the magic is giving him the feeling it's not going to end," Gideon explains patiently, his attention back on his LEGO.

My stomach flips. "It does that?"

"Sometimes," Sam admits. "It's not like it's promising you and Garrett are going to be in love forever. But I'm getting a really good feeling about your marriage. So… for now, at least, don't worry so much."

Hope makes my chest tight, but I nod. "Enjoy my time with Garrett. I can do that."

ᔕᗰ

I GO STRAIGHT BACK to Hortplatz. I told Garrett I'd be a little late, and he assumed it was for work, which makes me feel guilty. So the first thing I do when I walk out of the teleport room is announce, "I went to visit Gideon."

"What?" someone—I think it's Micah—calls from the kitchen. "Is that you, Ash?"

I glance around the empty hallway. Maybe the guilt made me just a little anxious. I should probably tone that down. "Yeah," I reply, heading in that direction.

He's alone, cutting himself a piece of cake, and I ask, "Where's Garrett? And where'd that cake come from?"

"One of Garrett's students. They must really like him at the school, because one of the kids showed up here this afternoon with her mother to deliver this extremely excellent cake." He leaves the cake and knife out as he sits at the counter with his plate. I take that as a sign to help myself to a piece.

"And where's Garrett?" I cut a smallish slice. Better to taste it first before committing to a big piece.

"He's back at the school. Something about Carol? Do we even know anyone called Carol?"

My memory kicks in. "Oh—no, it's not a person. Part of that whole human Christmas thing is that they sing songs and call them carol." I think. And he did tell me they were going to do a carol thing at the school tonight. I take a bite of cake and make a sound of pleasure. It really is excellent.

"Told you," Micah says. "This is my third piece. If you being married to Garrett means we get quality baked goods like this, you're just going to have to stay married to him."

I chew and swallow. "Working on that." Not that we'd live here with him and Zac forever, but I can worry about that later.

Micah's choking on cake crumbs, and I put down my fork for long enough to thump him on the back. It's very satisfying, so I do it again.

"Yeah, okay, enough!" he gasps. I pick up my fork and return my attention to the cake as he sucks in a breath. "Did you say you're going to stay married to Garrett?"

I scrape up the last of the frosting and let it melt into my mouth. "I want to. Guess we need to see how he feels about it. I'm giving him time."

Micah pulls a face. "Time to realize he wants to stay married to you? That seems kind of overconfident."

"Gee, thanks."

"What if we just don't let him leave? In winter it's easy enough, and when the road clears, we could do something to his car."

I slowly put my plate down and turn to look at him. "Are you suggesting that we illegally imprison him here? I don't think that's the type of marriage I'm really looking for, thanks all the same."

"Not imprison," Micah protests. "We wouldn't lock him up or anything. We just wouldn't let him leave."

I sigh and get up to put my plate and fork in the dishwasher. I want more cake, but not if it means having to listen to Micah spout this crap. "You should stop and think about what you just said. Think really hard. And know that if Enforcement ever came looking for you, I'd turn you in without hesitation."

Leaving him sputtering in the kitchen, I teleport to the school. The carol thing should still be going, and I want to show Garrett that I support him in every way.

CHAPTER TWENTY-ONE

Garrett

One Saturday afternoon in January, Zoe and I are adding details and suggestions to the growing list of things to be considered if non-demons are going to live in Hort-platz when we hear raised voices. She stops talking midsentence and glances at the door. "Do you need to check on that?"

We're having this meeting in my office at the "teachers' house," so I know it's not Asher and Zac arguing over the remote control. "I'm not sure." I listen, rather than just hearing, and realize that the voices aren't just Annie and Sid. "I think I do."

I'm on my feet and halfway to the door when it bursts open. Asher's standing there, face pale and set, even for a demon. "Is Isaac here?"

I blink. "Isaac? No. Why…" It dawns on me that if he's asking, with his expression like that, it means Isaac isn't where he's supposed to be. "He's missing?"

Asher's curt nod sends my stomach plummeting to my feet. "We're putting together a search party," he says. "First here in the village, then…" He doesn't finish the sentence.

If Isaac's not in the village, he's wandered further into the mountains… on a cold, lightly snowing evening in winter. If we don't find him, exposure will kill him quickly.

My heart clutches at the thought of the adorable, cheeky little boy lost and exposed to the elements.

"How can we help?" Zoe asks.

"We're going house to house to see if anyone's seen him, if you want to—"

"Yes," she says, and Asher nods at her.

"Thank you. My cousin is making copies of Isaac's picture. Do you know where my aunt and uncle live?"

"Isaac's parents? Yes. He always waves from the window when I clear the road in front of the house." She pales slightly. "Is this my fault?"

"What?" I ask. "How would it be your fault?"

"He's too little to teleport yet, right? So… if I wasn't clearing the roads, would he have been able to get out at all?"

"It's not your fault," Asher assures her firmly. "We didn't keep the kids locked up before you came, and this isn't the first time one's wandered off in winter. They find a way."

Looking slightly reassured, Zoe leaves.

"Let me get my coat and stuff," I tell Asher. "How're your aunt and uncle?"

He leans against the doorframe. "Panicky but trying not to be. They thought he was playing in his room, so they're not even sure exactly how long he's been gone." He swallows hard. "I didn't want to say, but… normally when a kid sneaks out in winter, they never make it that far because the snowdrifts slow them down."

But because we've been clearing the roads, it's easier for them to get around now. "That doesn't mean he's left the village," I insist. "If anything, the big drifts outside are more likely to keep him in. But let's go find him."

ⓂⓂ

THE VILLAGE ISN'T that big, and we have a lot of volunteers helping, so it's not long before we know nobody's seen him. That's not a surprise—with the way demons teleport everywhere, avoiding going out into the cold, unless someone happened to be looking out a window that faced the right way at the right moment, it was unlikely anyone would see one little boy.

But we've searched the village from end to end, and he's nowhere to be found. We head back to Micah's parents' house, which is being used as the base for the search, to prepare to venture outside the village.

His mother is a wreck, though to anyone unfamiliar with demons, she'd look only mildly upset. Damaris is hovering beside her, face absolutely livid. I'm not sure who she's angry with—the situation, maybe?—but I'm going to stay out of her way just in case. I feel so helpless, though—I don't know the area, so I can't contribute much right now, with everyone poring over maps and trying to decide which way Isaac would have gone. It's already getting dark, and the light but steady snow has already concealed his footprints, and I can't help wishing he'd decided to do this last night, when it was clear.

There's no point wishing for stupid things, though. I inhale deeply to steady myself, taking comfort from the hints of Isaac's scent that permeate his home—

Fuck me. "I'm so stupid," I say out loud, getting every-one's attention. Sure, I'm used to ignoring my sense of smell, but I *know* hellhounds are often called in for search and rescue because of how good we are at smelling things. Clearly I don't think fast under pressure.

"What?" Damaris asks, and the word is loaded with a threat. I try to ignore her, taking another deep breath, then turning to Hilda, Isaac's mother.

"Could you get me something of Isaac's? Maybe the shirt he wore yesterday, if it hasn't been washed, or his pillowcase?"

She blinks at me in blank confusion.

"What the—" an angry voice starts, but Zac's shout of comprehension drowns them out.

"Yes! Yes! Aunt, go, find something, quick!" He crosses the room in long strides to reach my side. "Do you think you can find him?"

The energy in the room shifts to hope so fast, it's painful. Hilda races out of the room.

"I don't know," I say honestly. "I think there's a good chance, but I'm not trained to use my nose. But I can try, and if I can't, we'll call someone who is. Alistair." Dammit, why has it taken this long for my brain to start working? "He's trained. We should call him."

"It's snowing," Micah points out, somewhat desperately. "Can't you try, at least get a hint of which way he went? Even if Alistair comes right away, we're still going to lose precious minutes."

He's right—I know enough about scent tracking to know weather is a big factor. I nod. "Yes, of course." But the doubt is heavy now.

Asher's arm slides around my shoulders. "You can do this," he murmurs, too softly for anyone else to hear. "I have faith in you."

My nerves steady a little. I *can* do this. Just because I haven't been trained to track by scent doesn't mean I can't smell where Isaac has been. My nose automatically does that shit all the time. Hellhounds have the best sense of smell of any species, and I'm taking things in that I don't even register half the time. The more I concentrate now, the stronger Isaac's scent is in this room.

Hilda runs back in, waving several small items of clothing and a pillowcase. "I brought everything that hasn't been washed yet," she says breathlessly, thrusting them toward me. I lift the whole lot to my nose and inhale deeply, and the concentrated scent is like a punch. My olfactory senses do their thing, sorting and filing all the scent markers, and then I exhale and go to the front door, snagging my coat from the rack before letting myself out into the cold night.

I slog in a circle around the snowy front yard while Asher and Zac hold everyone back at the door. There are a lot of fresh scents here, with so many people having come and gone in the past hour. It's frustrating, and my brain is overwhelmed and confused. I'm so used to just ignoring or even actively trying to block out smells that I can't process this.

On the verge of giving up, I turn back to the house... and see all the scared, hopeful faces watching me. Unbidden, Isaac's face that day he bumped his head rises in my mind's eye. He was distressed then, and he's probably distressed now. Cold, alone, and scared out there in the snowy dark.

There's no way I'm giving up. I can do this. Hellhounds have the best sense of sme—

That's *it*. I don't know why my brain is working so slowly tonight, but I'm glad it's catching up. I shift into my canid form, and instantly the scents are a hundred times clearer. It's also easier to process them in this form.

There are a lot of traces of Isaac here in the yard, most of them older, but here...

Inhaling deeply, I let my instincts take over. It's definitely from today. Someone with training could say how many hours old it is, but I just know it's today. I shift back and call, "Did he come out this way before he went missing? That you know of?"

"No," Asher's uncle Hal calls back, voice shaky with hope. "We went to the store this morning, but we teleported. Otherwise, he's been inside all day."

I nod, shift again, then take a few steps forward, following the scent through the gate. It's muddled there by all the people who've come through since, but when I turn my head to the left, I get a stronger waft. So I go left.

Then stop. I have his scent. I need to stop *trying* and get this done so we can bring him home. I go back into the yard and shift back to biped. "Grab what we need. I've got it."

There's an outburst of excited sound, then bodies scramble every which way. Asher comes down the steps to me. "I'll grab your gloves and hat. Give me those, too. Will you need them?" He nods to the tiny shirts and pillowcase still in my hands.

I look down at them, only now realizing how cold my hands are without gloves. I'm not even sure where I left them—usually I put them in my coat pocket, but they're not there. "I don't know. Maybe—could you put them in a bag or something?" I rack my brain for any details of scent tracking I might have been told over the years. "In a plastic bag. A Ziploc one if you can find it." That will protect the scent.

"I'll find one," he assures me, then leans in for a kiss. "Thank you."

"I haven't done anything yet," I remind him, not wanting to get hopes up. There's every chance I'll lose the trail, especially if it keeps snowing.

"You've given us a direction. We weren't even sure if he'd gone out the front door or the back," he points out. "You've done a lot, and I bet you're going to do a lot more." He kisses me again, and I take a second to just bask in it—not only the kiss itself, but the accompanying approval and appreciation. The unflinching respect I get from Asher is nice. Other people respect me too, but with Asher, I can count on it. There's no doubt in my mind that he'll support me.

When we're not so preoccupied, I should probably give that some deeper thought.

People start pouring out of the house, and Asher goes to grab what we'll need. Zac comes to stand with me. "I'm going to keep everyone behind you, with just me and Asher with you," he says. He sounds weirdly focused and professional, but I guess he's the most obvious choice to be in charge of a search party in the mountains, since he spends so much time there and is the unofficial village ranger. "I've managed to convince most people to stay here, but we need a good-sized group in case we run into problems." The set of his mouth turns grim, and I try not to think about the kind of problems we could run into in the snow-laden mountains at night. "We have a two-hour time limit," he continues. "I can't justify having people out in these conditions after that." His voice cracks on the last word, and I know it will kill him if he has to make the decision to leave Isaac out there.

"I'll move as fast as I can," I promise. "I'm going to be in hellhound form—is that okay?"

He thinks about it. "That may slow us down. We don't have snowshoes for dogs—we've never needed them. The snowshoes will already slow us down. I wish we could teleport, but there's too much ground to cover out there and no way to know where we're going."

Fuck. A tiny eddy of panic rises in me. Can I follow the trail in biped form?

I push it down. *Let's just see how it goes.* I can follow the trail through the village easily enough, since Zoe cleared the roads. When the snowdrifts start piling up, I can decide which form is faster.

Asher comes out, the last to leave the house, and hands me my gloves and hat. "Let's go."

CHAPTER TWENTY-TWO

Asher

GARRETT LEADS us quickly and without hesitation through the village, and I try to tamp down my hope. If this doesn't work out, I can't show him my disappointment. He'll already be wrecked and blaming himself—I won't add to that burden.

But we seem to be off to a good start. I glance over my shoulder to the rest of our search party, lagging about fifteen feet behind. Zac might not have to use his search and rescue skills too often, and I don't think he's worked with scent-tracking canines since he did his training, but he remembers what's needed. He laid down the law with our relatives, only letting those of us with SAR training who swore we could control our emotions come along. Grandmother snapped at him, and he banned her from coming. A lot of people underestimate Zac because he's so easygoing and disappears outdoors a lot, but if anyone can get Isaac home safely, it'll be him.

We reach the edge of the village, and Garrett doesn't pause, plunging into the snow without hesitation. Zac was concerned about this, and I was too, but we failed to take into account that we're following Isaac's trail, and he has little legs and no snowshoes. He's taken the easiest path, and Garrett has no problem following him in canid form—if anything, it seems like it might be easier for him because his weight's distributed over four feet instead of two. Whatever the reason, Zac and I exchange a glance of relief and pick up our pace to keep up.

After twenty or so more minutes, Zac says, "Hold up a minute," and pauses. We're in the woods now, which has made things simpler because the trees provide a lot of shelter. "Garrett, is the trail still strong? Still leading in a straight line?"

Whoa. I hadn't noticed that, and as Garrett huffs and nods emphatically, I look back toward the village. It's too far and too dark for me to be able to see it, but in the light of our torches, I can see that the tracks we've left are almost in a straight line. There's some minor veering around trees and the like, but Isaac definitely wasn't wandering aimlessly.

"Is he going somewhere?" I ask. "What's even out this way?" If I remember right, we'll start climbing within the next hundred or so feet, and then the trees start thinning. Surely he'll turn off before the tree line.

"Micah, Uncle," Zac calls, gesturing, and they hurry forward to join us.

"What is it?" Uncle Hal asks eagerly.

Zac explains, then says, "If he continued in a straight line like this, he's somewhere higher on the peak. There's nothing up there, so I'm guessing he turned off before then. Can you think of where he might have gone? Could he have doubled back?"

Uncle shakes his head in bewilderment. "I'm not even sure why he came this way. He doesn't like the woods—says they're scary."

"Every time we come this way, he holds my hand," Micah agrees. "I don't think he would have stayed in the trees longer than he had to."

"Damn," Zac says. "Does that mean he's trying to get to something on the peak? What's he doing?" He sighs heavily. "Let's try calling him. It's safer here in the trees—once we get out into the open, it'll be too risky."

Hortplatz's unique location means the village is rarely at risk from avalanches, and Zac keeps a careful eye on things to reduce the risk even further. But we often hear the telltale rumble of avalanches vibrate through the alps in the winter—and especially in the spring. Every year, Zac teaches an avalanche safety and survival course, and it's mandatory for everyone over eight in the village.

I haven't heard anything like that tonight, and the conditions aren't right anyway, so I resolutely push away thoughts of Isaac being caught unawares by a deadly mountain of snow, and join the others in calling his name.

We call, wait ten seconds, listening desperately for a response, then repeat the calls. There's no answer.

"Let's keep on," Zac says at last. "If he's above the tree line, we'll have a better chance of spotting him against the snow, even in the dark. And he'll be able to see our torches." He doesn't mention the driving wind up there, or how few places there are for even a small boy to take shelter.

Our trek becomes steeper very quickly, but the trail is still unerringly straight. Garrett pauses a few times to circle, and once he changes back to biped.

"Isaac's scent is stronger here, kind of puddled. I think he stopped to rest, maybe sat down for a few minutes."

"In the snow?" Micah whispers, glancing back toward where his dad is with the rest of the group. "He must be so cold."

"He's still moving, though," Garrett assures us. "And

his scent is a little stronger, even with the snow falling. I think we're gaining on him."

He shifts back before anyone can reply and bounds off in the direction Isaac is going. We follow.

When the trees start to thin, Zac calls another halt. We can see clearly to the windswept, snow-laden rock ahead, and there's no little boy in sight.

Garrett shifts into biped form. "It's going to get trickier now. The wind and heavier snow are fucking with the trail."

"Can you get any direction?" Zac asks, waving the others forward.

"Unless he changes direction suddenly, he's still going mostly straight." Garrett hesitates. "Maybe veering a bit to the left now. Let me just…" He changes to canid form and takes off so fast, I yelp.

"He shouldn't go alone," I say, taking three quick steps after him before Zac grabs my arm.

"He's already on his way back."

Sure enough, Garrett is loping back to us. He skids to a stop in the snow, shakes himself, then changes to biped and points. "He's veering that way."

I squint, trying to orient myself better. "Aren't there caves over there?"

"Caves?" Garrett asks sharply. "Did he know they were there?"

"All the kids get told there are caves in these mountains and they need to stay out of them unless there's an adult with them," Zac says. "I don't know if he'd know specifically about these caves… but it looks like he's headed straight for them."

Micah growls. "He knows. This is my fault. We were up here last summer gathering wood for a bonfire. He was talking a lot, asking questions, and I ended up showing him one of the caves. I don't know how he remembered which way to go, though. Especially with all this snow. I'm so sorry."

"But why would he want to go to an empty cave?" Uncle Hal asks. "In this weather, after dark? Why didn't he turn back?"

I shrug. "We can ask him later. This might be good news, right?" I look at Zac. "If he's in a cave, he has shelter."

Zac's face is grim, but he nods. "Which cave?" he asks Micah. "Could you teleport there and check?"

"Yes," Micah says, then glances around at the snow. "Maybe. I haven't been up here in winter." There's a momentary crackle of teleport energy, but it's off, and Micah goes nowhere. Disappointment is written all over his face, alongside the pain of a failed teleport.

"There must be too much snow piled up around the entrance," Zac consoles him. "Walking won't kill us. Which cave?"

As Micah describes the location of the cave, I sidle up beside Garrett, who looks like he wants to cry. "What's wrong?" I murmur. "We're going to get him back." I slide an arm around him.

He takes a shaky breath. "This might be my fault. I told him a story once about a dragon living in a cave…"

"Don't be foolish."

I blink and turn my head. Uncle Hal has come up beside us and obviously overheard Garrett's comment.

"Uncle—"

"No. There will be no more apportioning of blame. Isaac knows not to leave the house without an adult. Hilda and I should have checked on him instead of just assuming he was in his room where he was supposed to be. Micah shouldn't have shown him the caves, Garrett shouldn't have told him a story… do you hear how ridiculous this all is? There is no fault. Children have imaginations and poor decision-making skills. That's part of being children. Now let's find him and take him home."

On that loud, decisive note, he strides out of the relative shelter of the sparse trees, heading upward and to the left. We scramble to catch up, the wind shoving at us and making the whole thing very uncomfortable. This is why I'm an investment banker—to avoid the wind and snow.

Even with the weather hindering us, it doesn't take long to find the cave Micah showed Isaac. We stumble inside with our torches, calling his name.

It's empty.

He's not there.

"No," Micah breathes. "He has to be here. Isaac!"

My heart clutches at the thought that he's lost somewhere out there. We're grown men and we struggled in that wind—how did he manage? Is he even now lying in a snowbank somewhere?

Zac rubs the back of his neck. "We didn't see any sign of him on the way," he says. "But we were so sure he was here… and the wind and snow would have hidden them. So we retrace our steps and see where we lost his trail. Garrett—"

"I can't smell him here," Garrett affirms. "But I kept getting hints of him on the way. I think he might have gone off track slightly? It was hard to tell… the wind…" He's still beating himself up despite what my uncle said, and I wish we had time for me to wrap him up in my arms and reassure him. But as long as Isaac is missing, he wouldn't listen anyway.

"You take the lead," Zac orders. Garrett shifts, and we follow him out of the cave back into the howling wind.

I keep my torch pointed at the ground, sweeping it

from side to side, looking for any sign that Isaac came this way. For all that the wind and snow feel horrendous, we're actually really lucky with the weather—it gets much worse up here in winter. Even in summer, the wind is like this. Garrett's sniffing madly, and every once in a while, he pauses, but whatever he smells must be fleeting.

Then, suddenly, his head comes up and snaps around.

"Do you have something?" Micah asks desperately, and Garrett makes a sound that I can somehow tell means "shut the fuck up." We stand there in silence, staring at him as the wind tears at our clothes and makes our eyes water.

When he goes from stock-still to running flat-out, it takes us a second to switch gears.

"What—"

I don't know who said it, but it doesn't matter; we all run after Garrett, hoping this is a good sign. He leaps up onto an outcropping from the solid wall of rock rising above us, then growls and jumps back down, sniffing around it.

"Garrett?" I approach him slowly, but he ignores me, still nosing around the rock.

Then I hear it. A child crying, the snatch of sound almost drowned out by the wind.

"Fuck! Isaac? Isaac!" Where is he? "Did you hear that?" I ask Zac.

He shakes his head. "No, but if you and Garrett did, that's good enough for me. Let's spread out along the rock face—"

Garrett howls triumphantly and disappears around the other side of the rock. I follow, tracking him with my torch… and watch him disappear into a crevice.

A crack in the rock face.

A fucking cave entrance, sheltered by the outcropping,

small and narrow and almost hidden from sight. It would probably be tough to spot even on a clear, sunny day unless you were right up close.

"Here," I call to the others, plunging after my husband. It's a tight squeeze through the gap, especially with my winter gear padding me out, but then I'm inside, my light falling on the most gut-wrenchingly amazing sight: Isaac.

Huddled against the cave wall beside the entrance, with Garrett licking the tears from his face.

"Puppy?" he asks, his little voice trembling, and then he looks in my direction, squinting. I point the torch up.

"Hey, Isaac. Did you get lost?"

His eyes widen as he takes me in. "Asher?" And he promptly bursts into tears.

CHAPTER TWENTY-THREE

Garrett

We all watch anxiously as Zac, the only one of us with medic training, checks over Isaac, who's clinging to his father like a limpet. He said he hurt his ankle, but from his and Zac's reactions as he turns it this way and that, I'm guessing it's not more than a minor sprain.

Thank fuck.

He's also cold, tired, and hungry, but since he so sensibly put on all his winter gear before leaving home, and with this cave offering such good shelter, he doesn't have any symptoms of frostbite. This is absolutely the best outcome we could have had, and I blink back tears of relief as I lean against Asher.

"I bet you're ready to get home," Zac says finally, smiling at his little cousin. "In just a few minutes, your mom will be giving you cuddles."

Oooh, yes. A benefit to being with demons—we don't have to walk home but can teleport. In just a few minutes, *I* can be making a cup of tea and having a hot shower. Bliss.

Isaac sniffles. "Okay, but you gotta bring me back

tomorrow. It was too dark for me to see all the treasure before."

"There's no treasure," Asher's uncle says gently. "That was only a story. There's just an empty cave."

The little face sets stubbornly. "No, there's treasure. I want to come back tomorrow."

"Isaac—"

Asher nudges me away and half turns toward the rest of the cave. "It's fine, Uncle Hal. Let's just shine our torches around so he can see there's— Fuck my life!"

"Asher!" several voices chide, followed by gasps and choked exclamations.

Because the cave isn't empty like we all assumed.

Near one wall, there's a line of wooden crates stacked five high. That's weird enough, but they're not the most interesting thing I'm seeing.

No, that would be the adjacent wall. The one that's a motherfucking cornucopia of gears and bolts and sliders, from the rocky floor all the way up twenty feet to the rocky ceiling.

How did we not notice how big this cave is?

And what the fuck is that wall?

"Um…" someone says. "What is that?"

"It's treasure!" Isaac pipes up. "Ed the dragon's treasure. He'll probably be back soon. I bet he's traveling with Billy the snow leopard."

Okay, I may not know what the wacky wall is, or those crates, but this, I can do something about. I go to kneel beside Isaac.

"Honey," I start softly, "I'm so sorry, but that was just a story. Ed the dragon doesn't exist. I made him up. I thought you knew that."

His eyes widen and his lower lip trembles. "There's no Ed?" he whispers, and I shake my head.

"No. I'm sorry."

"But… what about this treasure?"

"I don't know what this is"—or how huge a coincidence it is that he happened to stumble upon *this* cave—"but I know for absolute sure that I made up the story I told you."

"So there's no dragon called Ed?" he repeats, as if hoping to get a different answer.

"No. Well," I correct, "there might be a dragon somewhere called Ed. But they wouldn't be the same as the dragon in the story."

He looks devastated, and I feel like something someone scraped off their shoe.

"But," his dad adds in a deliberately cheery voice, "even if Ed isn't real, you still found something special here! We don't know what it is, but everybody's going to know you discovered it."

Isaac thinks about that for a second, and then his little chest puffs out. "I'm a discoverer!"

The sound Micah makes as he pats his brother's head is half laugh, half sob. "You bet you are. Now, how about Dad takes you home? People are waiting to see you."

Isaac nods, suddenly drooping with exhaustion, and turns his face into his father's neck. "Call me when you get back," Micah's dad says to him, and then he and Isaac teleport out.

I stand, and Micah and I go to join the others, who've moved closer to the crates and wall. They're going slow, sweeping the light along the floor and up to the ceiling.

"Looking for traps?" I ask, and Asher grunts.

"Zac thinks this might be a smuggling cache."

I look over at Zac. "Really? All the way up here? Isn't the nearest road down in Hortplatz?"

"I didn't say it was logical. But let's not take any risks."

He inches a little closer. "In fact, why don't we leave it for tonight? I want to come back with better lights and some other gear."

A very reluctant murmur of agreement runs around the group. We're all eager to see what's in those crates—and what the hell that wall is—but we're also tired, cold, facing an adrenaline crash, and working by the light of half a dozen handheld torches. Coming back in the morning with equipment is the sensible thing to do.

"Teleport marker?" Asher suggests, and Zac pulls out his smartphone and takes a couple of pictures of the wacky wall and the crates. Before I came to Hortplatz, I didn't know demons needed a visual reference before they could teleport somewhere. It makes sense, though—how can you go somewhere if you don't know what it looks like? Asher told me that some demons can even teleport to a *person*—but it's extremely risky.

Speaking of Asher... he looks around for me, then holds out his hand. Time to go home.

ԶՄ

It's stupid early when I wake the next morning. I can tell before I even open my eyes—the air has that stillness that tells me normal people are sleeping.

"You awake?" Asher murmurs into the darkness, his growly morning voice making me shiver with awareness. I guess he's about as normal as I am.

"Yep. Is it too early to get up and go back to the cave?"

My words hang in the silent room. We didn't talk about it last night—just came back to the house, showered, ate, stared blindly at the TV for a while, and went to bed. Micah went to his parents' house first, and when he got home, he assured us that Isaac was fine—already tucked into his parents' bed with a stuffed dragon and a nightlight, warm, fed, and fussed over. I'm sure we were all *thinking* about the cave, but none of us said anything.

Now, though… now, it's tomorrow.

"We need to wait for the others," Asher cautions. "Zac, especially. This falls into his domain."

"Maybe we should go make breakfast. Noisily."

He chuckles and rolls onto his side, slinging a warm, heavy arm across my chest. "What do you think it's all about?"

I sigh. "Zac's idea of a smuggling cache is the most logical. Probably not a current one, though. There used to be a village here before, right? Didn't someone tell me it was abandoned, and that's what made you all decide to build here?"

"Yeah. It was barely a village, though. About a dozen buildings in total. And it was abandoned over two hundred years ago—maybe closer to two hundred and fifty. Those crates would have rotted by now, wouldn't they?"

I shrug. "Maybe. I don't know enough about wood to say. It was pretty dry in there, though. Unless we open them and find something spectacular, the crates aren't as interesting to me as that wall, though."

"Hmm. What even was that? Was it… decorative?"

I blink into the darkness, then lean over to switch on the lamp. "Did you just ask if someone designed and assembled that wall to decorate a cave at the top of a mountain in the middle of nowhere that was being used for storage?"

He squints in the sudden brightness, then chuckles. "Yeah, I guess it's not likely. But what would all those gears and cogs and bolts do?"

Our gazes meet. I'm pretty sure we're both having the

same thought, but it's so fantastical and outrageous that neither of us wants to say it aloud.

I cave first (no pun intended). "Lock to a hidden chamber?"

"Why would anyone have a hidden room in a cave at the top of a mountain in the middle of nowhere… and then store their boxes outside it?" He throws my words back in my face, then sighs. "But it's gotta be the entrance to a hidden room."

We lie there thinking about that for a minute. The anthropologist in me is *thrilled*. Even if the cave and cache belonged to humans, this could be a fascinating behavioral insight. Especially the wall. A lot of effort went into that.

"When we go back, we should look to see if there was a bigger entrance at one point," I muse. "Something that got closed up by a rockfall, maybe. That would explain why things got left behind—they couldn't get them out." There has to have been a way they got *in*, too. Demons might have been able to teleport the crates in, but they also could have taken them out the same way, which makes me think there probably weren't any demons involved. Every other species would have had a hell of a time getting them up there, though.

Asher sits up suddenly.

"What?" I ask, following suit.

"What if the rockfall didn't close the entrance, it opened it?"

I cock my head. "Say what?"

"Think about it. The only way into that cave that we saw was the tiny crack we went through."

"Yeeeeahhh…?"

"So what if that's new, and the room we were in is the hidden one? The wall with all the cogs is the back of the vault door. We were *inside* the vault, and the main entrance is somewhere else."

Oooh. "Clever," I say admiringly. "The front side of the wall/door would be a lot more discreet-looking… like a vault door."

He jumps out of bed. "Okay, let's go clang some pans while we make breakfast. I can't wait too much longer."

I laugh at him as I clamber out from under the covers. "Aren't you finance types supposed to be all stodgy?"

He stops with one leg in his pants. "Garrett, there might be treasure in those crates. Actual treasure. The 'finance type' in me is dying to see for myself."

A frisson of excitement runs through me. I guess we're all treasure hunters at heart. "Do you think so? Treasure? Like… gold coins and jewels?" I grab a sweater. The house is well-insulated and heated, but it's still chilly.

"Maybe. Or maybe artwork. Historic artifacts. Who knows?"

I grin. "We will, as soon as we get up there."

DISAPPOINTINGLY, I don't have to wake my cousins with a lot of banging around. Zac's already up and has gathered a pile of equipment, including some huge battery-powered lanterns that look like they could light up a stadium. Micah's also up and chugging coffee.

"Whoa," Garrett says with a laugh. "Go easy on that."

"Can't. Need it to open my eyes."

"Go back to bed if you're that tired," I suggest, opening the fridge and staring at the contents.

"Can't," he repeats. "Zac's determined to leave in the next hour, and Isaac called at three thirty."

Garrett stops pouring coffee. "This morning? Why?"

"He wants to go back to the cave with us. Mom talked him out of it, but she said I'd tell him what was there. And then he turned that into me giving him a Zoom tour of the cave."

I snort and grab the eggs. "So he's no worse for wear, then."

Micah's only answer is to put his head down on the table.

I feel the tingle of a teleport. "Zac?" I call.

"Yeah! Gimme a hand with this."

Handing the eggs to Garrett, I head for the teleport room. Zac's there with a long rectangular box almost as tall as he is. "What's that?"

"The other half of the portable winch." He glares at the box. "It's so damn awkward to carry."

"Yeah, sure, *why* do we need a winch?"

The glare transfers to me. "Those crates were stacked five high, Asher. How were you planning to unstack them?"

I… had not thought of that. My face gets hot. "Well, you can barely balance your personal accounts," I retort. It's weak but true. Zac's talent does *not* lie in numbers.

Just like mine apparently doesn't lie in planning treasure retrieval adventures.

"Help me get this to the rest of the stuff," he orders, and I pick up one end of the box. The motherfucker is *heavy*.

"Why didn't you just take this stuff straight to the cave?" I huff as we maneuver out of the room and down the hall.

"Two reasons," he says, barely panting. Damn him for being so fit. "First, I didn't trust myself to just drop everything off and leave."

"And the other reason?" We make it to the living room, where the rest of the gear is stacked, and set the box down with a whole lot of relief.

Zac dusts off his hands. "I was pretty sure if I went there without you all, one of you would hurt me."

Hmm. "Possibly." Definitely.

We go back to the kitchen, where it smells like the eggs are nearly done and Micah is looking marginally more awake.

"What's the plan?" Garrett asks, getting plates out.

Zac sits at the table and steals Micah's mug. "Joke's on you," Micah gloats. "It's empty."

Rolling my eyes, I pour coffee for us both and top off Garrett's cup.

"Hey," Micah whines. "What about me?"

"Can you revert to childhood another time?" Garrett interrupts. "What's. The. Plan?"

Zac shrugs. "I just sent texts out to everyone who was with us last night to see who wants to come back with us. They have half an hour to decide and get ready, then we're going."

Garrett cheers and does a little happy dance. "Just wait until I tell Alistair I helped discover a treasure cave. He's going to be so devastated." The vicious glee in his voice makes me laugh as I help him dish up our breakfast.

"The first thing we'll do," Zac continues, "is set up the lights. Nobody touches anything until we have sufficient lighting to see what we're dealing with."

Garrett forks some egg into his mouth and gazes thoughtfully at my cousin. "I've never seen you be so authoritative before."

Zac shrugs. "Normally it's just me and the mountains. There's nobody to boss around."

Micah and I laugh so hard, I nearly choke, and Garrett passes me a glass of water with a raised eyebrow.

"Ignore them," Zac says. "They think I was a bossy kid, but it's not true. Asher was the bossy one."

"I'm the oldest," I protest. "I wasn't bossing; I was leading."

"Please stop," Micah gasps. "I can't breathe."

Garrett turns back to Zac. "Are you sure you want to bring them along this morning? Treasure discovery is serious business."

"Hey! I'm your husband." In a fit of pique, I grab the last bite of toast from his plate. "You're not supposed to want to leave me behind."

He smiles and leans over to kiss my cheek. "Sometimes it's necessary to leave you behind, but I never *want* to."

My stomach flips in excitement. He never wants to leave me? That's a good sign... maybe he's also thinking about making our marriage permanent. I just have to be patient and show him how I feel.

I clear my throat. "I don't want to ever leave you either."

Based on the way Zac coughs and Micah's eyes widen, that might have been a little intense. But it's okay. Garrett doesn't seem to think anything's weird.

"So you're going to concentrate on being a serious treasure discoverer? We have a responsibility, you know. It's up to us to reintroduce whatever's in that cave to the rest of the world. It could be a forgotten part of history. Or it could help solve a crime!" His face is alight with excitement. I'm not sure whether the most credit goes to the hellhound in him or the anthropologist, but sensible, calm Garrett is nowhere to be seen.

"I'll be a serious treasure discoverer," I promise obediently.

"Great! And when my name is on everyone's lips as the hellhound who changed the world, Alistair can suck it!"

"Changed the world?" Micah whispers.

"Just go with it." I smile indulgently at Garrett. "Whatever makes him happy."

꠵

WHAT MAKES him happy is helping to set up the lights, then insisting I take a picture of him grinning broadly and flipping off the camera, with the crates and the wall behind him.

"It's for Alistair… and my other cousins," he explains as he takes his phone back. "I'll send it when we get back to the village."

"Okay," Zac says, looking around the group. Uncle Hal stayed home, as did one of the others, so there are only six of us. "Here's how this is going to work. We check the crates first—visually on the outside, then we get a ladder and see if we can open one of the top ones. What happens after that depends on what we find inside. Everyone wears gloves, goggles, and a mask until we're sure there are no harmful substances." Although we're not as sensitive to toxins as humans are, they can still cause problems for us. "Everything that happens from now is being recorded." He nods toward the camera on a tripod that he set up, and then holds up his phone. "Are we ready?"

"What about the wall?" Garrett asks, pulling disposable gloves from the box Zac brought.

"Let's open at least one of the crates first, and then we'll get a closer look at the wall. If we're dealing with banned or dangerous substances, we're going to need to get the authorities in here."

"What if this is a human cache? We can't call in the human authorities," Micah counters, and I smack him on the back of the head before reaching for a mask.

"CSG has a department to deal with human shit," I remind him. "Don't you pay attention to anything?"

"Don't you dare start bickering now," Garrett warns before Micah can retort. "We have a mission." He turns to Zac. "I should be the one to go up the ladder and open a crate."

"No!" I immediately protest. "What if there's something dangerous in there?"

"Yeah, Garrett," Micah echoes. "If there's something dangerous in there, Asher would much rather his blood relatives who he grew up with get hurt instead of you."

Someone coughs, badly hiding a laugh, but I just look at Micah. Is he waiting for me to deny that?

"Asher," Garrett chides, and I sigh.

"Of course I don't want anyone to get hurt. Whoever goes up"—not Garrett—"will do this as safely as possible."

"That's why it should be me," Garrett says, damn him. "I can shift if there's a reason to worry and jump down a lot faster and more safely than any of you can."

I hate that he's right.

"Let's look at the crates before we decide this," Zac says, adjusting his goggles. "We haven't even got that close to them yet. I've got this gadget that detects known poisons and toxins, and it's going to have the final say. Could be that nobody's going up the ladder." He glances around. "Everybody got their safety gear?"

Micah leans over to me. "We're going to lock him outside later, right?"

"In his underwear," I agree. Garrett's hellhound ears must hear us, because he glances over and tsks, but he's smiling.

Zac picks up a fancy-looking handheld doohickey with a lot of buttons and a little screen, starts filming with his phone, and leads us toward the crates, heading for the ones at the farthest end from the wall.

The crates are big—about three feet by three feet—and made of wood, though I have no idea what kind. They look sturdy and in good condition. Garrett's right; it's pretty dry in here, and I guess that makes it good for storage.

A sudden beam of light hits the nearest crate, and I jump, startled, until I realize Zac's turned on the flashlight on his phone. "No toxins detected yet, and it doesn't look like there's any writing on this side," he says, running the light over the entire side of it and leaning closer. "If I had to guess the type of wood, I'd say some kind of pine… maybe. It seems to be well made." He walks around it, shining the light on the two other sides we can see. "No marks or stamps… does anyone else see anything?"

We murmur in dissent, then follow closely as he moves down the row, inspecting the crates we can easily see—the bottom two rows. There's no writing or maker's mark on any of the crates, unless it coincidentally happens to be on the sides we can't see. Zac keeps pausing to hold his gadget close to the crates, especially near the seams, but nothing happens, and he doesn't start yelling for us to get away.

So far, treasure discovering is a lot more boring than investment banking. At least when I'm working, there's the potential risk of losing thousands or even millions of francs. Right now, I'm just standing around looking at boxes while wearing a costume similar to when we were kids pretending to be the Scarlet Pimpernel. At least then I got a pretend sword… when Micah didn't whine so much, I had to let him use it.

That reminds me… when we tell Gideon about this, we have to make it sound a lot more exciting.

"Okay," Zac says finally. "Let's get the ladder."

Garrett's racing back to the pile of gear before he even finishes speaking. As I watch him pick up the folding ladder and carry it back, I realize I have two options: I can physically prevent him from going up that ladder, or I can bite my tongue and try not to panic to death while he goes up.

I narrow my eyes. He's almost as big as I am, and hellhounds are sneaky… could I even manage to hold him back?

He gets back to us and sets the ladder down. I can't see

his mouth behind the mask, but his eyes are smiling. Then he sees that I'm looking at him. "Don't even bloody think it, Asher. You try to keep me from climbing this ladder, and you'll learn the true meaning of blue balls."

Panic to death it is.

CHAPTER TWENTY-FIVE

Garrett

Despite my threat to Asher, there's a tiny part of me that wishes he would try to stop me. The rest of me squashes it like a bug and helps Zac set up the ladder. This is exciting, and I can't wait to see what's in those crates.

Zac hands me his phone. "Can you record and climb the ladder at the same time?"

I take it dubiously. "Probably… but do we really need to record the rungs as I climb?"

"No, but there might be something on the crates that the video will catch," he explains patiently.

With a big sigh, I start recording and put my foot on the first rung. "I can manage it."

Asher appears at my side—not that he's been that far anytime in the past few minutes. I get the feeling that he's still struggling not to throw me over his shoulder and whisk me somewhere else. He'd better not if he knows what's good for him, but I love that he wants to. It makes me feel special… protected. I've never liked overprotective, possessive partners before, and never thought I wanted one, but there's something about Asher that's different.

Garrett and Asher, sitting in a tree, K-I-S-S-I-N-G...

The little voice sounds a lot like Alistair, and I tune it out. I have an important job to do now. Getting all swoony over my hot, masterful, maybe-not-so-temporary (crap crap crap, I just thought it) husband can wait for later.

"Be careful," Asher says in his growly voice that makes my dick perk up. "If you see anything odd, get down right away."

I chuckle and kiss him through both our masks. "Odd like this whole situation? It's fine, Asher. I'll be careful." Without giving him time to say anything more, I turn and scramble up the ladder, trying to keep the phone steady and pointed at the crates. At the top, I turn on the phone's flashlight to get better visibility. There are some shadows up here.

Tracking the light over the lid of the top crate, I feel a thrill of anticipation. "There's a symbol on this one," I call down to the others. "I don't know what it means, though." It's on one of the far corners, and I lean across the crate to see it more clearly. The black ink is clear and dark, not faded much, if at all. These crates can't have been here that long—there's not even a lot of dust on them.

"Be careful!" Asher yells, and someone—probably Micah—repeats it in a high-pitched voice, mocking him. This whole thing about demons being scary and unapproachable is clearly a myth.

Except Damaris. She still makes me want to wet my pants sometimes, and I'm pretty sure she likes me now.

"Garrett, take a picture of the symbol and text it to Asher," Zac calls. "Let's see if we can recognize it before you try opening."

Obediently, I stop recording, snap a picture, and open the messaging app to send it to Asher... which proves easier said than done. "I can't find Asher's name in here," I tell Zac.

"Yeah, he's in there as The Boring One."

"You're such a dick," I hear Asher say as I find the right contact. "I'm not boring, I'm financially gifted."

"You're boring," Zac and Micah declare in unison.

"Trust me, he's really not," I call down to them, frowning at the screen. We're all so stupid. "The text won't go through." Because we're in a cave at the top of a mountain and there's no service up here. Which we all *knew*, but somehow forgot in the past two minutes. "I'm coming down." I know Asher, and probably Zac too, will have a hissy fit if I open the crate without checking the symbol first, so I slide down the ladder like I've seen people do in movies. It's fun!

Asher's yell of alarm warms my heart, but less so when he snatches me off the ladder with a jolt.

"You ruined the landing," I complain as he mashes my face into his chest. The words are muffled, but I stamp my foot—unfortunately, right on top of his—and that seems to get my disapproval across, because he lets me go.

I look up to scold him some more, and the big idiot is smiling. A demon-size smile, but still. "You're so violent," he marvels. "It's kind of hot."

Um… what? And they say hellhounds are weird. Ignoring him—maybe I accidentally kicked him in the head when he grabbed me off the ladder?—I turn to Zac and hand over the phone. Everyone immediately crowds around.

"I've never seen that before in my life," someone announces.

"Zac, go home and internet search it," Micah suggests. "We'll wait here."

Zac's laugh is loud and derisive. "Like I'd trust you all here without me. You take it. Try to be quick."

"Yeah," I agree, trying to look casual as I lean back against the ladder. In actual fact, I don't want anyone getting bright ideas about it being "their turn." I'm going to be the discoverer of what's in the crates. It's my destiny.

Muttering about how we better not have any fun without him, Micah teleports out. "Let's look at the wall while he's gone," Asher suggests. "That'll piss him off."

Zac bites his lip, torn between sticking to the original plan and doing something that will infuriate one of his cousins. I feel his pain. "Fine," he concedes. "But we do it carefully. And I need someone else's phone to record with."

Asher hands over his, then, as we make our way closer to the wall (I hang back until everyone's moved away from my ladder), enthusiastically fills the group in on the theory that we're already *inside* a secret room.

"Maybe," Zac says. "Assuming this is a door."

"What else could it be?" one of the others asks, and I realize with a little start that I don't know his name. We were in a search party together and now we're in the same discovery team, but to me, he's just a random demon. Whoops.

Guilt trickles through me. I haven't spent as much time socializing and getting to know people as I should. I know all the families associated with the school pretty well, since I made a concerted effort to do that, and of course Asher's family and their intimates are part of my inner circle— which is a little frightening. But outside of them and a few others at the bar and the supermarket, I don't really know anyone in town. I've been too wrapped up in the school and Asher and trying to find a point of attraction about the village that will make other species want to live here.

That has to change.

But not right now. First… the wacky wall. Later, I'll make friends.

Zac stops three feet from the wall, prompting the rest of us to stop too, and shines his light on it. Up close, we can see some minor—very minor—rust on some of the metal pieces.

"You'd have noticed if people were using this cave since you moved here, wouldn't you?" I ask Zac.

He shrugs. "Depends. If they were moving crates like that in and out and had teams of people here, yes, definitely. Even if I didn't see them, I'd have seen signs of them. But one or two people who know what they're doing, just stopping by to check on things? Maybe not."

"What if the entrance to the cave is miles away, down a long tunnel on the other side of this door?" Asher asks. I raise an eyebrow, and it's his turn to shrug. "What? It could happen."

"My point," I say, turning back to Zac, "is that you've been here for over fifty years and never knew about this cave. Can we assume this has been abandoned for longer than that? I thought it hadn't been that long, since there's not much dust on top of the crates and they're in good shape, but I guess if the cave was mostly sealed… and it's very dry in here too."

"I guess. I didn't want to make an assumption like that just yet. Even as dry as it is, this isn't a lot of rust for fifty years." He plays the light over the closest metal components, then frowns. "Huh."

"What?" the rest of us chorus, and I choke down a giggle.

"I thought these bits were all screwed into the rock, but they're not." He takes a step closer, and we all follow suit. This close, it's easy to see he's right, even without the bright light. There appears to be a backing between the sticky-outie components and the rock wall… Wait. Is there even a rock wall? Fumbling out my phone, I turn on the flashlight and hurry along the wall to the end, where the last of the components is, where it meets the adjacent wall.

"Garrett?" Asher follows me. "What are you doing?"

I run the light up along the corner, looking for any sign—

"There!" I reach out and prod the tiny, millimeters-wide gap. It's not completely visible, I'm guessing because of passing time and lack of use. "It's a door. Definitely a door. It's not part of the cave wall at all—it's blocking off a tunnel or another part of the cave."

The others join us and see for themselves. Once you know what you're looking for, it's obvious that there's a seam, though it's a pretty good fit.

"Let's check the other side," Zac says.

It only takes a minute, and then Asher sighs. "Dammit. This proves my theory wrong."

I frown. "How so? It's still a door."

"But the hinges are on the other side," he points out. "Nobody puts hinges on the outside and then locks the door. It's stupid."

"Unless you're trying to keep something inside," guy-I-don't-know points out, and as one, we turn to look at the crates.

So of course, that's the moment Micah teleports back in, scaring the crap out of us all. Zac yells, and someone (maybe me) throws their phone at him. But I'm not great at throwing, so it just hits the cave floor between us.

"What the fuck?" Micah demands, scowling. I'm too busy trying to get my heart rate back to normal to care about how scary he looks.

"You better not have cracked the screen," I snap, flouncing over to pick it up.

"Me? You're the one who threw it. Why would you do that? I thought we were friends."

As I pick up my phone, dust it off, and check it for damage—none. That case was worth every penny—Zac explains what's happened since he left.

"So those crates might contain something smart enough to know how to take a massive door off its hinges?" Micah asks. "That have lived in boxes without food or water for probably more than fifty years?"

"Well, when you put it like that..." Asher concedes. "Did you find out what the symbol means?"

He shakes his head. "Similar stuff came up, but it was all for fiction books and some movies. And nothing exactly the same."

I take a deep breath. "I'm going up."

"Maybe—" Asher starts, but I shake my head.

"Nope. Let's do this." This time, I'm the one who leads the way to the ladder. I take Zac's phone, start recording, and climb. Then I immediately climb back down. "Did we bring like a crowbar or something?"

"I'll get it," guy-I-don't-know says, and I take advantage of his brief absence to lean over and whisper to Asher.

"What's his name?"

My husband blinks at me, then says, "Lon."

Lon returns with the crowbar. "Here you go."

I smile at him. "Thanks, Lon." Asher makes a choked sound as I turn back to the ladder.

This time, when I reach the top, I'm ready. I balance the phone on the second rung from the top, wedging it against the side rail so it stays upright and the camera can mostly see what I'm doing. Then I test a few places around the edge of the lid, find a likely spot, and put the crowbar to work.

The lid comes off a lot more easily than I expected. I definitely needed the crowbar—especially since the ladder doesn't allow me a lot of leverage—but I didn't need to strain at all. It pops right up, and I grab it, adjust my grip, and push, sliding it back to rest on the crate behind. With the crowbar gripped firmly in hand, I peer into the crate.

CHAPTER TWENTY-SIX

Asher

WAITING ANXIOUSLY, I put my hands on the ladder. If Garrett gives even the slightest indication that things aren't okay, I'm ready to shove it out of the way and catch him.

"What's in it?" Micah calls impatiently.

"Metal bits," Garrett says, his voice puzzled. "Like the ones on the wall. Do you think they were planning to expand it?"

"I thought we'd decided it was a door?" Lon asks. "How do you expand a door in a cave?"

By blowing up the mountain, I think, and turn an alarmed look on Zac. He must be thinking the same thing as me, because he shakes his head. "The reader is calibrated for explosives. There aren't any in this cave."

"Come down," I call up to Garrett. Zac might have confidence in his reader thingy, but I've invested in enough new tech to know that things are being invented all the time. Who's to say that the explosives in these crates aren't some kind of super-advanced product his gadget wouldn't recognize?

Except… they would have needed to travel back in

time to be hidden in this cave more than fifty years ago. So… maybe not.

Still, I'll feel better once Garrett's on the ground. "Bring some pieces down for us to see," I add, so it doesn't seem like I'm being overprotective. Which I'm not. "Overprotective" implies a lack of reason, and I'm absolutely being reasonably protective.

To my relief, he starts shoving things into his pockets, then climbs back down the ladder. We crowd around him.

"Here, look at these." Garrett pulls out five different metal pieces. One's a cog, there are two bolts of different sizes, and some other things I don't know the names of. "The crate is sectioned into compartments, and each one had a different type of part in it. There must be at least a few thousand of each of these."

Micah takes one of the bolts and studies it. "It can't be to expand the wall," he says, almost to himself. "Why would you want to…"

We wait.

And wait.

"Why would you want to what?" Zac asks finally. Micah doesn't respond, just staring at the bolt, so Zac elbows him in the side.

"Ow! What?"

"Why would you want to what?" Zac repeats.

"Why would I want to what, what?"

"I'm going to kill you," I threaten him, and he shakes his head.

"But I haven't done any—"

"Okay," Garrett interrupts, catching hold of my arm. "Let's all just calm down. Angry people on a frozen mountain is how documentaries about murder get made, and I don't want to be in one." Before I can work out what he means by that, he turns to Micah. "Before you started thinking so hard we could smell smoke coming from your brain, you said 'why would you want to…' So now's the part where you tell us what you were thinking about."

Micah pulls a face. "It's a theory. It might be wrong. It's definitely farfetched."

"As farfetched as this?" Garrett waves an arm at the crates and the wall.

"Maybe. Let me just…" Micah takes off toward the wall.

"If he leaves one more sentence unfinished, I'm going to finish him," Zac mutters to me as we follow.

Micah stands in front of the wall… door? What should we be calling it? He seems to be studying the pieces of metal. Finally, he reaches out, takes hold of one piece, and pulls.

Nothing happens.

So he tries twisting it.

"Micah, what the fuck? Don't break it," I caution. Once we figure out what or where the key is, we want everything in working order.

"I'm not going to break it," he says in a heavily condescending tone. "You forget that I'm an architect and an engineer, Asher. This kind of design comes *naturally* to— Fuck me!"

We all stare, not sure what to say. While he was giving his self-congratulatory little speech, he tried sliding the piece, and it moved.

"Was it supposed to do that?" Garrett asks.

Micah nods. "I think so." He slides the piece back to its original position, then tries sliding it in a different direction. "I think… I think this might be a puzzle."

"Like, you're puzzled?" Zac asks. "We're not surprised by that."

"No, you idiot. Like a mechanical puzzle. I don't think there's a key for this door, I think the door *is* the key."

I put my arm around Garrett and tug him closer as I try to work that out. "So you have to solve the puzzle to make the door open?"

"Yes. I think."

"When you say mechanical puzzle," Garrett starts, "do you mean one of those handheld puzzles where you have to move the parts in a certain sequence?"

Micah nods, relief crossing his face that one of us understands. "Exactly. They have different levels of difficulty. Some you just have to move the parts in the right order. Some you have to move the parts a certain way in the right order. And some…" He turns back to the wall. "…you have to work out where the extra pieces go, and in what order, while moving the existing parts in the right order."

"Fuck me," Lon says. "Just thinking about it gives me a headache."

"Yeah, this one is kind of big and complicated," Micah admits. "If I'm right about what it is, we're going to need an expert."

Dammit. "Do we think someone's gone to this much trouble and expense to create such a complicated key to a door in a cave at the top of a mountain in the middle of nowhere just because?" I ask, and get a lot of blank looks.

"That's a complex sentence," Garrett says at last. "But I'm going to go with no. If this was just a fun puzzle they were in the mood to create, they'd have done it close to home. There used to be a settlement where Hortplatz is now, right? Any chance those people did this?"

"No," Micah replies. "It was tiny and not that sophisticated. Plus, I can't see how they would have gotten this stuff up here nearly two hundred and fifty years ago, if we couldn't easily do it today."

"They could have built the crates in the caves and carried in the components a few at a time," Lon suggests, but he sounds doubtful.

"So the more likely option," I say, bringing things back on track, "is that someone went to a lot of effort and spent a lot of money to hide something up here."

A murmur of reluctant agreement goes around the group.

"Which means…"

"…we have to report this," Zac says. "We have to hand the whole thing over to the government."

He sounds about as disappointed as I feel. Our exciting adventure amounted to looking in a box and finding some spare parts. Garrett's face is a picture of tragedy, but he squares his jaw.

"It's the right step," he insists. "We don't know what's behind the door or even if the door is booby-trapped. I'm not willing to risk that we might blow up half this mountain and injure the children in the village. Not to mention," he adds, "I have to go in to work tomorrow and won't have time to play with the puzzle."

I stifle my chuckle. "Think of it this way. You get to ruin your cousin's Sunday by making him come out to a frozen mountain and look at bits of metal." Because when you've got connections at the top of the government, you don't call the local Enforcement office. Which is miles down the mountain anyway.

That cheers him right up.

"Let's get the winch set up and unstack the crates," Zac suggests. "Maybe there's something in one of them that will give us more clues. And this way, we'll have more photos to send to Gideon and Alistair, because you know they're going to ask for them."

We all agree a little too quickly. Nobody's ready to let go of the adventure just yet.

🙢

"WHAT THE ACTUAL fuck did you find?" Gideon grumbles, swiping through the photos on Zac's phone. He's in a shitty mood and has been since I called and told him he had to bring Alistair and come out here on his day off. Apparently this is the first weekend in about six weeks that Sam hasn't had work obligations, and Gideon's not thrilled to be called away. We've already been up to the cave so they could see everything in person, and now we're sitting at our kitchen table, looking at the pictures in more detail.

"And why didn't you call me sooner?" Alistair adds in an injured tone. "I can't believe you hogged this to yourself, Garrett. You've always been selfish."

A growl rips from my throat as I turn toward him, but Garrett pats my arm, grinning wide. "He's just being a sore loser, Asher, because I am the king of treasure discoverers and he's just another hellhound."

The gasp Alistair gives is worthy of a Hollywood movie, and for a second I think he's going to swoon like a golden-age heroine. He even puts the back of his hand to his forehead. "You take that back," he whispers dramatically.

Garrett just smirks gleefully. "Prove me wrong."

"Alistair, I swear if you don't stop fucking around and pay attention, I am going to kill you, and I don't even care how mad Sam will be," Gideon threatens, and for a second, we all gape at him. He won't care how mad Sam will be? He must be at the end of his tether.

Like a switch has been flipped, Alistair is suddenly in professional mode. "So the crates had different combinations of items, but some of them were repeats. Like there were bolts of the same size in four different crates."

I shrug. "So?"

"When you match that with every crate having a different symbol on it, I'm guessing the components have been laid out in the order they need to be used. The reason they didn't put all of the same items in the same crate is because to open the door, you'll need, say, a dozen of that item at one point, but then won't need the rest until later. Whoever did this was trying to make it easier to open."

"You agree it's a door, then?" Garrett asks, and Alistair and Gideon exchange a glance.

"Almost definitely," Gideon says. "You did the right thing calling us before you tried to open it. We'll get David out here to see if there are any wards or sorcery booby-traps, and then some specialist equipment to see if we can get a sense of what's on the other side."

Whoa. "Wouldn't we have sensed any wards?" I ask. I haven't spent that much time around sorcerers, but I did hire some good ones to put up wards at my apartment and office in Zurich. Since I'm not always there, it seemed like a sensible precaution. I always feel the gentle tingle of those wards when I walk through them.

"It depends on what the wards are supposed to do," Alistair says. "Sometimes they need to be hidden."

Garrett glances up at me with wide eyes. Suddenly the precautions Zac made us take don't seem like they were enough.

CHAPTER TWENTY-SEVEN

Garrett

PART of me is hoping that Alistair's trying to get back at me for saying he's just another hellhound, but the rest of me knows he's not. Not yet, anyway. I'm sure his revenge is in my future.

"Okay," I say, trying to sound breezy and not like being the one to open the crate might have been the dumbest fucking decision of my life. I slide my hand down Asher's arm and take his hand. "So step one is to have someone check for wards and booby-traps, step two is to scan through the door to what's behind it. Then what?"

"Depends what we see behind the door," Gideon says. "If it's an empty room, nothing. If there's stuff there, we'll try to get the door open. My preference would be to blast it, because decoding that stupid puzzle will take forever."

"No!" I gasp, echoed by Alistair and Micah.

"No way," Micah adds. "That puzzle is one of a kind, and it's a masterpiece. You can't blast it."

"Do you know anyone who can solve it?" his cousin growls back.

"I do," Alistair sings.

"You do?" I blink at him. "Really?"

"Of course really! I wouldn't make up a thing like that." He's back to using his "I'm hurt and offended" voice. "I can send him the pictures right now and get an opinion, if you like."

"Do it," Gideon orders before I can reply. "I'll call David and get him out here to check for wards." He glances across the table at Asher. "Does Grandmother know what's going on? Or Jesse?"

Silence. I stare at the tabletop and try to be invisible.

"Maybe before we call in anyone else, you better let the village council know."

"Now that we've advised the proper authorities, isn't that your job?" Zac asks hopefully.

Gideon laughs. "Nice try."

Well… fuck.

ֱֱֱ

"Walk us through this again," Jesse says an hour later. Asher called him and said we needed an emergency session of the village council, and to his credit, he got everyone together fast. I'm not sure how I was elected to go along with Zac and Asher, though.

"Yes." Damaris's tone is low and dangerous. "By all means, let's clarify."

Zac's eye twitches, but my glorious husband looks unfazed by his grandmother's ire.

"When we located Isaac last night, the cave he was in wasn't empty," Asher begins.

"We understand that part," Damaris interrupts. "Why wasn't that reported to the council immediately?" And by "the council," she means her.

"There were other priorities." Asher stands his ground. "We were all cold, tired, and hungry. We'd been out searching for nearly two hours in the snow and wind."

"Of course," Jesse soothes. "Your personal well-being took precedence. But, uh… this morning, when you decided to go back to the cave and collected quite a bit of equipment to do so…" He gestures to the wall-mounted TV where Zac's photos are on display. "Why didn't you advise the council then?"

"It was very early still," Zac says. "And we weren't sure whether it was even worth disturbing the council over. My plan was to have a look in the crates, see what was there, and then come back and report."

You don't need to be a vampire judge to know that's a lie, but despite some skeptical looks, nobody calls him on it.

"And once we realized it wasn't just an old hunter's cache," Asher says smoothly, "we called in the appropriate authorities and came to tell you immediately."

"Did you not consider that you should have come to us first and allowed us to call the authorities?" Damaris asks.

"We were trying to save time?"

I give Asher props for not cowering, but he loses points because it sounds like a question.

"Regardless of the proper protocol," Jesse says, clearly trying to prevent bloodshed, "things are in train now. What happens next?"

"Gideon will take a sorcerer up to the cave to check for any hidden traps or wards," Zac volunteers. "We're still not sure if this was made by humans or the community, so the policy is to check. They should be here soon. And Alistair, Garrett's cousin who works with Gideon"—there's a ripple around the table. Most of these people were at our wedding. They remember Alistair—"knows someone who makes mechanical puzzles. He's apparently a master and should be able to open the door."

"Until that's done and the contents of the cave are identified and catalogued," Asher continues, "it's considered to be a restricted CSG site. They want to minimize the chances of anyone getting hurt in there."

Damaris's eyes narrow. "Are you saying we, the council, can't visit this cave and see for ourselves what all the fuss is about?"

Asher almost trips over his tongue rushing to say, "I'm not saying that at all." His grandmother gives a satisfied nod, and he winces before adding, "The Community of Species Government is saying it."

Her face darkens, and a murmur of discontent rises from the rest of the council.

"I'm sure Alistair and Gideon would be fine with you having a look. They just don't want everyone from the village wandering up there," I suggest, mentally kicking myself for opening my mouth as all eyes turn to me. Asher's gaze asks me what the fuck I'm doing. "Let's give them some time to sort out the details, and then you can request an escort."

For the first time since Asher and I announced our engagement, Damaris turns her "I'm going to murder you" look on me.

"An escort?" she hisses.

"To answer your questions. Not for any other reason." Sweat breaks out along my spine.

"Thank you," Jesse announces, and as the attention moves away from me, I suck in oxygen. "We'll discuss this and decide what steps we want to take next. Please advise Gideon and Alistair that we'd like to speak with them before they leave."

I hardly hear the exchange of farewells before I latch onto Asher's arm and let him teleport me home.

I'm barely oriented to being in the teleport room—and swallowing hard to keep my lunch down—when Micah yells, "That you?"

"No!" Zac calls back, then leads the way to the kitchen. Where he stops in the doorway for me to run into the back of him.

"Dammit, Zac, I'm still all dizzy. Why are you trying to make it worse?"

"Move or I'll move you," Asher threatens him, even as he gently steadies me.

"Sorry, I wasn't expecting us to have company," Zac says over his shoulder, moving into the kitchen so we can get through.

"Company?" I look toward the table and see who he means. Gideon, Alistair, and Micah are there, of course, and I recognize the newcomers from my wedding. David Carew and his boyfriend, the elf Caolan. "Hi. Good to see you both again."

David stands politely and offers his hand. "You too. Married life agrees with you."

Alistair grins wide and opens his mouth, but Caolan elbows him, and then they put their heads together and whisper furiously. I can hear them, of course, but they're not saying anything worth listening to.

"We were just waiting to hear how the meeting went before we take David to the cave," Gideon says.

"Grandmother isn't pleased. The council wants to speak to you before you leave." Asher's words are simple and informative, but the underlying tone is a mix of resignation and gloating. Damaris is mad at everyone right now.

"Great," Gideon mutters, but Alistair perks up.

"I didn't get a chance to meet your grandmother at the wedding," he exclaims. "I'm *dying* to."

I wince. Alistair's annoying, but he *is* still my cousin. "Now's probably not the best time for chitchat," I warn. "Keep it professional."

He solemnly traces his forefinger in a cross over his heart. "I swear by all I hold dear."

My face must still show my doubt, because David says, "I'll go along and keep an eye on him."

"Thank you," I tell him over Alistair's yelp that he's perfectly capable of being professional, fuck us all very much.

"Okay, let's get moving," Gideon interrupts. "I want to get home to Sam at some stage this week."

"Are we all going?" I ask hopefully. Now that CSG is taking over, I'm not sure if I'll get to go back to the cave after this. Gideon and Alistair speak at the same time.

"No."

"Sure!"

They look at each other, then glance at David.

"As long as you obey orders, it's fine," he says. "Have you ever traveled by portal before?"

I blink at him. "Teleport, you mean? Sometimes, with Asher."

He shakes his head. "No, I mean by elf portal. Don't worry, you'll love it. It's a lot better for non-demons than teleporting."

"Excuse me?" Asher says, inexplicably offended that I might like some other form of travel better than teleporting, which still routinely makes me sick. I pat his arm.

"Let's wait and see. But even if I like it better than teleporting, you'll still be my favorite."

He doesn't seem all that mollified, although a minute later, after Caolan has looked at a few of the pictures we took in the cave and opened a glowing doorway right there in the middle of the kitchen, Asher's jaw drops.

I study the portal thoughtfully, and when it's my turn to go through—with Asher clinging to my hand—I brace myself. It's needless. I feel nothing. It's like stepping through a regular doorway, except the other side is miles away.

"Hey, guys?" I say casually to Alistair and Gideon as we wait for the others.

"Hmm?" Alistair asks, his attention already on the wall.

"If you knew elves could do this portal thing, why didn't you mention it any of the times people were talking about how Hortplatz gets cut off in the winter?"

For a second, nobody reacts. Then Alistair, Gideon, and Asher all turn to stare at me.

"Just think," I continue. "You hire *one* elf and set up a public transport schedule of portals to Zurich or wherever. Portal opens at nine fifteen, a dozen people go through, and voilà. All done. No need for a demon to teleport back and forth to help multiple people."

"I'm feeling distinctly underappreciated," Asher mutters. Alistair looks like someone slapped him with a fish. I quite like it.

"Not all elves can make portals," Gideon says finally. "Those who can are in high demand for government jobs."

"All of them?"

He shrugs, and I make a mental note to talk to Caolan about this. Maybe there's a semiretired elf out there somewhere who wants to make some extra cash by opening a portal a few times a week. They wouldn't even have to live here, since they can just portal here when they need to.

Caolan steps through the portal, and it closes behind him. "Big fan of your work," I tell him. "That was an amazing travel experience. Five stars."

He grins. "I like you, Alistair's cousin. Wanna be bros?"

Yeeeeahhh… he's definitely spent too much time with Alistair. But it would be rude to refuse, right? "Sure. Come up next weekend for the snowman contest, and we'll hang out."

"A snowman contest?" He turns to David. "Did you hear that? They're having a snowman contest! Can we come?"

"We'll probably need to check on things by then anyway," David murmurs absently, gaze skimming around the cave. "This is extraordinary. Where's the entrance?"

Zac shows him, and Alistair sidles up beside me. "Why didn't you tell *me* about the snowman contest?" he asks in an injured tone. I was the one who taught him that tone when he was a pup, so it has no effect on me.

"How were you going to get here?"

He puffs out his chest. "My bro Caolan would have brought me."

"Okay, but more importantly, why would I invite you anywhere after you nearly ruined my wedding?"

"I was *protecting* it!" he yelps. "But hey, while we're on the subject—"

"You're clear through most of the cave," David interrupts as he and Zac come back. "I'm not getting anything from the crates, either… which is just as well, since you've already rummaged through them."

"We didn't know wards existed that could be hidden so thoroughly," Zac protests.

"Let me just check the wall, and then we'll see if we can scan through it."

"Have we called Brandt yet?" Caolan asks.

"Who's Brandt?" Micah mutters as we look toward the elf examining the crates.

"Why are you asking us?" Asher hisses, and I elbow him. No need to take his mood out on others.

"We haven't," Gideon says. "Why would we need to call Brandt?"

Caolan points to the symbol on the lid of the crate he's standing beside. "Because that's an ancient dragon numeral."

CHAPTER TWENTY-EIGHT

Asher

"It's a *WHAT*?" David demands as Alistair crows loudly. Beside me, Garrett gasps, and when I look at him, he has his hands clasped under his chin and an expression of utter delight on his face.

"It's a dragon treasure hoard," he says. "I am the discoverer of a dragon treasure hoard!"

"Technically, Isaac would be the discoverer," Micah says, then clamps his mouth shut when I glare at him. If my husband wants to be the discoverer, he can be the discoverer. Isaac will be thrilled just to be named as part of the group.

"Isaac's the team leader," Garrett allows, his sense of fair play showing up. "Now, hush so I can listen."

"Here," Caolan says, tapping the symbol. "It says four." He glances down the line of crates. When we unstacked them, we were careful to keep them in the same order, and this one is in the first—formerly top—row, fourth from the left. He takes two steps to the next one and peers at the lid. "And this says five."

David joins him. "I know dragon numerals," he

protests. "Dragons use the same numerals as elves. That's not a five."

"I said *ancient*," Caolan reminds him. "I can't remember why, but for a few millennia a long time ago, they used different numerals. To be fair, I only know this because I was on one of the teams helping to move archives after the world started coming apart. We were shown what all of them meant so we wouldn't accidentally miss anything. I think even some dragons wouldn't recognize them."

I frown. I don't know a lot about dragons, but aren't they big? We'd have noticed a dragon coming and going from here, right? And if they were in biped form, they'd pretty much have to come through Hortplatz. There's no other road up this mountain.

"Well, that certainly makes this a lot easier," David says with relief. "Let's call Brandt and have him send a dragon out to take a look. I wouldn't be able to recognize a dragon ward anyway."

"I might," Caolan offers, "but I'm not seeing anything. Wait… it's not a ward, exactly." He squints at the wall, then turns that same look on the boxes. "I'm not sure what it is, but a dragon definitely magicked all this."

"Is it dangerous?" I demand. Garrett was the first to open a crate, and everyone who's ever watched a movie knows the person who breaks the seal cops the worst of the curse.

The elf shrugs. "I'm trained to recognize dangerous magic, so no. I don't know what it does, though. The dragons have some weird spells, and because of how their magic works, sometimes the normal stuff looks different."

I have a feeling asking for more information would lead to a long and complicated conversation that I won't understand, so I just nod.

Garrett's cousin opens his fat mouth. "How is it diff—"

"Let's worry about that later," Garrett interrupts, probably because I started growling. It was involuntary, I swear. I don't think I could take Alistair—he's trained in combat, and I'm trained in finance.

I could tank his credit rating, though.

"If calling Brandt is the best step to take now, we should do that," my sensible, sexy husband continues. "Brandt would be… oh, you mean the dragon species leader? That Brandt?"

"Yes," David confirms. He pulls out his phone and sighs. "I guess we need to go back to the village to make the call."

Caolan smiles indulgently at him. "I can take you to him, love. For you, I'll do anything." He pauses. "Well, almost anything, which is why we'll go to the front gate and wait for someone to let us in. The security at the dragon estate is excessive."

"Can't argue with that," David mutters.

"Should we go back to the village and wait?" Zac asks, but David shakes his head.

"No. If I know Brandt, as soon as he hears about this, he'll come to look for himself. We won't be long."

They leave moments later, and Garrett wanders over toward the wall. "I discovered a dragon treasure hoard. Although… it hasn't been that long since the dragons came back to Earth, right? How did Zac not notice a huge dragon coming and going from here?"

"Maybe the dragon has an elf friend who portaled them in," Zac suggests.

"Even if they don't, you probably wouldn't have seen them. Dragons have this spell that conceals them from sight," Alistair informs us. He sighs. "Sometimes I really wish I had magic like that."

"We're all glad you don't," Gideon says. Alistair glares at him and goes to stand with Garrett. They put their heads together and begin murmuring.

"This is so surreal," Micah says. "I can't believe this whole thing was built by a dragon. Sometimes I still don't believe dragons are even real."

"Oh, they're real," Gideon mutters darkly. "And they love karaoke."

I try not to shudder as I cast a glance at my husband, who is a fiend for karaoke. "So they're like hellhounds?"

He nods. "They get along like a house on fire. Or worse, like fur on fire. Which happened a lot in one of their stupid little games."

"You know," Micah muses, "we might want to consider trying to attract dragons to live here. They could come and go as they please because they can fly."

"No." Gideon shakes his head. "You don't understand. They will drive you *insane*. I don't even know how you cope with the hellhound living in the same house."

"I beg your pardon?" My voice is cold, and I prepare to defend my husb—

"Just throw me up there, Alistair! It's fine if you don't catch me; bones heal."

Gideon raises an eyebrow, and I sigh. Hard to defend that. "No throwing," I call. I'm the one who'll have to look after him while he's healing, and I'm a terrible nursemaid.

"But I want to see the ones near the top!" Garrett pouts, and I feel myself weakening.

"The ladder's still here," Zac points out helpfully, and as the two hellhounds scramble for it, I glance gratefully at him.

"Thanks."

He shrugs. "I don't want a pouty broken hellhound in

the house, either. But should they be putting a ladder against that wall before the dragons check it?"

"We touched it," Micah points out. "It's probably safe to touch."

I doubt Garrett will listen if I try to stop him, so I just call, "Be careful!" as they prop the ladder against the wall/door and start bickering over who gets to go up first.

"That's not going to end well," Gideon sighs. "If Alistair breaks his stupid head, Sam's gonna yell at me."

"Really?"

"After he yells at Alistair," he amends. "Sam's fair that way." He strides toward them, and we watch as he confiscates the ladder.

"Can't touch the wall until we know it's clear. You know better, Alistair." He brings the ladder with him as he rejoins us, a smug expression on his face. Behind him, both hellhounds are glaring at his back.

Micah's gone back to gazing at the wall/door. "Do you think the dragons will let me examine the puzzle when it's solved? Because the engineering involved must be incredible. I'd love to meet whoever designed it."

"Maybe you can," Zac suggests as I wander to the nearest crate and peer inside. "You can both geek out over engineering and bits of metal."

The sound of their conversation fades from my notice as I move among the crates, looking at all the different parts. Micah's right: this is incredible. I can't even begin to imagine how these pieces could be added to the existing base to unlock it. Honestly, I can barely differentiate between some of the parts. Micah says there are six types of bolts, but I only see three. The other three are so similar, I don't see a difference.

"…I'm *married*, Alistair!"

It's the hushed hiss of Garrett's voice that cuts into my

introspection, but the words definitely get my attention. I lift my head, realizing I'm only about six feet away from them now.

"Yeah, I know," Alistair says, his voice lower than usual but not enough for me not to hear him. "But we all know that's just a temporary thing. And this guy is perfect for you, Garrett, but he's also great in general. I'm not sure he'll still be single when you get around to ending your marriage."

For a second, I just stare in shock, but then rage roars through me. Alistair can't seriously be trying to set *my* Garrett, my *husband*, up with someone else, can he?

And Garrett's not thinking about it, is he?

I'm on the verge of leaping forward and strangling Alistair from behind—even if he is likely to win in the end, I should get a few good hits in—when the only remaining sensible part of me paralyzes every muscle, freezing me in place.

Alistair's right. Our marriage is temporary… officially. I might be trying to turn it into something more, but Garrett doesn't know that. Attacking his cousin probably isn't the best way to convince him I'm the person he wants to be bound to for the rest of his life.

"I'm not saying you've gotta have an affair," Alistair continues, and part of my ire fades. Not much, but a tiny part. "Just let me introduce you online. You guys can chat as friends, and at least that way, when you and Asher split, Tony will know you and probably be ready to step in."

The ire comes back. I stand there, mostly frozen in place by my own overwhelming feelings, wondering if it would count as murder for me to tell Grandmother about this and then let her handle it. I mean… technically I'd be able to tell Garrett I had nothing to do with it, right? And nobody would ever find the body, anyway. We could just tell people he ran away with the circus, and everyone who knows him will probably believe it.

"Alistair, that's… I was going to say sweet, but it's actually really weird." Garrett pats his cousin on the arm. "Did you get hit in the head recently?"

"Why do people keep asking me that?"

Probably because they all want to hit him in the head. I know I do.

"Well, anyway, as weirdly kind-of sweet as it is that you're thinking of me, I've been thinking that I might see if Asher's interested in staying married for longer than we discussed."

The words are a wonderful, glorious, amazing slap in the face. As the shock of victory reverberates through my body, I wonder if now is the time to let them know I'm listening.

"Really?" Alistair's doubtful tone stops me. I'm definitely going to mention him to Grandmother. I'll also tell her that he annoys Gideon, her favorite. She's guaranteed to do something about him then. "You want to stay married to the demon banker who lives in the middle of nowhere? I didn't really mean it all those times I called you boring, but now I'm starting to wonder."

Garrett shrugs. "There are downsides—a lot of them —to living here, but I still like it. Mostly. Plus, Asher spends a lot of time in Zurich, which is lovely. And… I don't think I'm going to be ready to let him go in just a few months." He pauses. "It might be possible that I'm falling in love with him."

Yesssssss! I open my mouth to shout it, but only the tiniest squeak comes out. I may need to seek medical help after this—I thought my response to shock would be a lot better than it is.

"It might be possible? Trust me, if you loved him,

you'd know." Alistair's supercilious tone turns dreamy as he says, "I *knew* I was in love with Aidan."

"Did you? Truly? Because that's not the story I heard."

"Pfft. What are stories, but retellings of events?"

Garrett nods. "Yes. That's exactly what they are."

"See! I'm retelling it differently from everyone else."

There's a momentary pause, and I can tell Garrett's wondering if it's worth calling his cousin an idiot. He must decide against it, because instead he says, "Well, whatever your story is, I know I love Asher. He's sweet and considerate and sexy, and he's always thinking of me. Being around him makes me happy, and when we're both at work, I miss him. It still seems like it's too soon to say I'm *in* love, but I do love him, and I think we'll get there."

"You're an idiot," Alistair declares, and I finally unfreeze all the way.

"Hey! Watch yourself when you talk to him," I snap, stomping over to them. They both whirl around, eyes wide.

"A-Asher," Garrett stammers. "I didn't see you there."

I wrap him in my arms and lay a big, wet kiss on his beautiful mouth. "I love you. And I'm *in* love with you. I want to stay married to you forever. If it's too soon for you to be sure, that's okay. I can be patient… as long as we're married while you work it all out."

He stares at me in shock as I pause to take a breath. "Oh, and we can live wherever you want. If you need to go back to Cambridge, I can commute from there, no problem. And if you need to study demons in the village, I'll make them all cooperate."

"You and what army?" I hear Micah say, but I ignore him. The most important person in this cave right now is in my arms.

"So… take your time deciding what you want to do, as long as I can keep loving you in the meantime. And I'd appreciate if you'd let me maim your cousin a bit." I keep my plot to have Grandmother murder him to myself. There's no need to give away secrets.

"That's not nice," Alistair protests. I barely hear him, too busy staring into Garrett's pretty brown eyes. "I'm on your side. I was just about to tell him that it sounds like he's already in love with you, just too boring and stupid to know it."

I growl and start to turn toward him, but Garrett grabs my face between his hands and pulls me into another kiss. When he finally lets me go, we're both breathless.

"I love you," he says. "I'm in love with you. I'm in love with my husband. This is amazing!"

The sound of someone clapping breaks into our happy declarations. "It certainly is! David, you never mentioned anything about this. We would have moved faster—I love a good romance."

CHAPTER TWENTY-NINE

Garrett

"I didn't know it was happening," David says dryly as I extricate myself from Asher's arms—keeping hold of his hand—and turn to see the newcomers. Aside from David and Caolan, there are two dragons. At least, I assume they're dragons. They have the same nonhuman features as Caolan, but there's something… different. "Nobody was making passionate declarations of love when I left. Can't I leave you in charge for twenty minutes?" David asks Gideon.

Asher's cousin shrugs. "I took the ladder away from them. The love thing didn't seem that dangerous. Also, I wanted to see my cousin make a sappy fool of himself."

"Not a sappy fool at all," the older dragon says. He's the one who spoke before, and he's smiling delightedly. "I want to hear all about your romance—I sense there's a story. But perhaps first we should…"

"Yes, of course." I drag Asher away from the wall. "It's such an honor to meet you. I'm Garrett Smythe. Professor Smythe. I wonder, could I make an appointment to speak with a dragon at some point? I have so many questions."

The words tumble from me in an unprofessional deluge, and I hear Alistair snicker behind me.

"Smythe?" the other dragon says. He's got dark hair and eyes and a suspicious expression that seems to be carved into his face. "You have the same name as Alistair?"

"We're cousins," Alistair says, coming up beside me and slinging an arm around my shoulders. "Garrett's cool, Stef. He's an anthropology nerd, so he'll have a lot of questions, but he'd never hurt anyone."

The dragon still looks suspicious, but a tiny bit of the intensity fades. His gaze skims past us to the wall/door. "What the actual fuck?"

"What the actual fuck, indeed," the older dragon, who I assume is Brandt, murmurs. "I never would have imagined…" He shakes his head.

"Can you identify who it belongs to?" David asks, and Brandt laughs.

"Yes, but I'm afraid that doesn't help. The dragon who created this was one of the first who ceased to exist during the anomalies on our world."

I frown, trying to process that. "But… I thought that before you all migrated, no dragons had come here for a long time." We were told the dragons and elves stopped visiting at the time of the species wars, about nine thousand years ago.

Brandt nods. "That's correct."

"Fuck me," I breathe.

"I don't get it," Zac confesses.

"If the dragon who made this died before the migration, and none of them came to Earth between the species wars and then, that means—"

"Fuck me!" he shouts. "You're saying this is *nine thousand years old*? No way. It's dry in here, but those crates would have been dust millennia ago." He sucks in a breath and calms down. "But that does mean I didn't miss the signs of someone coming and going from this cave."

Asher snorts, coming up beside me, and I lean against him. Partly for support after this shock, but also because we're in love and going to stay married. I get to spend the rest of my life with Asher.

"Actually," Brandt says, "it's significantly older than nine thousand years. I'd say closer to fifteen."

Now I'm leaning on Asher because my knees have gone weak.

"As far as the crates go, both they and the door are protected by excellent preservation spells. They can't completely stop aging, but they slow it down a lot."

"A whole hell of a lot," Asher says, voice heavy with awe. I glance toward the crates, which look like they were made within the past decade. Are they really so old?

"Can we hand this over to you, then?" David asks, and my stomach sinks. I hadn't thought of that—if this all belongs to a dragon, we don't get to play with it anymore.

"Nope," Brandt says cheerfully. "Finders, keepers. It's going to take an expert to solve this puzzle, and I don't want that headache."

Steffen, who's moved a little closer to the door, says, "This is a work of art. Not just the puzzle, but how the preservation spells are woven in… I wish I could have met the dragon who designed it."

Brandt snorts. "You would have loved her. Her wards and booby-traps were exceptional."

"Speaking of booby-traps," Micah says. "Are there any?"

"Yes," Brandt and Steffen say at the same time. Brandt continues, "But they'll only go off if you try to force the door."

"What about explosives?" Gideon asks. "Did they even have those back then? Or if we tunnel around the door?"

Steffen shakes his head, grudging respect on his face as he studies the door again. "I wouldn't risk it."

Gideon swears, but Alistair claps his hands. "Cam is going to *love* me."

Brandt smiles at him. "Who?"

"Alistair has a friend who makes mechanical puzzles," Steffen explains. "Did you call him?"

Alistair nods. "Yes, but I had to leave a message. I sent the pictures, though, so I'm sure that as soon as I'm back in cell range, I'll hear from him."

"Well, that all works out for the best, doesn't it? We can leave this safely in the hands of CSG." Brandt smiles beatifically.

David smiles too, but it's not happy at all. "Nice try. The contents behind that door belonged to a dragon and now belong to their next of kin... or failing that, to you as the dragon government."

"She has no remaining family," Brandt protests. "And I don't want the bother of..."

As they argue over who should be in charge of opening the door, I get an idea. A wonderful, brilliant idea. I turn my head and whisper to Asher, "How much does your grandmother love you?"

He blinks at me. "Maybe a bit less, after today. Why?"

"I need her to not kill me, please." Before he can ask anything else, I raise my voice and interrupt the argument. "Could I make a suggestion?"

Everyone turns to me. "By all means," Brandt says. "Suggestions from hellhounds are always good."

If anyone else had said it, I'd think they were being sarcastic, but he looks genuinely eager.

"Thank you. Um... do we know what's behind the

door? In a general sense, I mean. Is it a dragon hoard?" And do dragons hoard treasure?

Brandt shakes his head. "Unlikely. We dragons like to be close to our hoards and have easy access. The top of a mountain might seem like an excellent place to hide your most treasured items, but unless you live nearby, it means you don't get to play with them much."

"Could your friend have lived nearby?" Steffen asks. "How old is the village?"

"Not that old," David says dryly. "The oldest continuous settlement in the world is only about eleven thousand years old. And it's not here."

"It doesn't have to be continuous, though," Steffen argues. "A good place for a settlement is a good place for a settlement, even if people come and go."

"Not so much in these mountains," Zac says. "Plus, it was colder fifteen thousand years ago—where the village is now was carved out by a glacier back then."

Micah stares at him. "How do you know that?"

Shrugging defensively, Zac replies, "I'm a geologist and I spend most of my time outdoors on this mountain. I was curious about how it used to be. Besides, we did a ton of research before we moved the settlement here. That's how we picked the village name."

"How so?" I ask, even though we're getting off track. I find details like this fascinating.

"This whole part of the mountain has been referred to as Hortplatz for nearly a thousand years," Zac explains. "Longer—that's as far back as it's documented, but there was a strong oral tradition in this area, and the records I saw estimated that it goes back a lot further. So it seemed right to name the village that."

"Hortplatz," Brandt repeats. "Your village is called

Hortplatz. Because this part of the mountain was known as Hortplatz."

David sighs. "Is this going to make me want to hide under my bed?"

"*In* the bed, not under it," Caolan corrects. "I'll come with you." His wink seems inappropriate for the situation, but I still find it sweet.

"No," Brandt assures him, ignoring Caolan. "I don't think so. It's the syllables that got my attention. Languages changed a lot between the last time we visited here and when we migrated, but a lot of sounds are the same. And back then, we swapped words back and forth a lot. Some of your Earth languages are loosely based on ours."

"Really?" I breathe. I no longer care that we've moved away from the point. This is fascinating. But then I realize what he's saying. "I thought it was a German word I just didn't understand." My German is sketchy to begin with, and place names in any language can often not make sense, since so often they're named after people or events.

"What?" Gideon asks.

"Hortplatz," Brandt says. "It has its roots in some dragon slang from a long time ago. *Hort* is literally hoard. It's very likely my friend is the one who named this area, way back when."

As my mind both struggles to absorb that while also doing a happy dance over the history of it all, Asher says, "So this could be her hoard?"

Brandt makes a face. "It still seems unlikely. This door… she did love puzzles, but even if she knew every move off by heart, it would take days to get the door open. We dragons love our hoards, and I can't imagine her being okay with that kind of delay. But, while I don't think this was her personal hoard, I do think she was hoarding something here."

"And that something would have the same preservation spells as the door and the crates?" I venture, remembering why I brought this up in the first place.

"I can't guarantee it, but I don't see why she'd protect them and not the contents they're guarding," Brandt agrees.

I nod. "Okay… so I propose this. The village of Hortplatz will coordinate the opening of the door and the cataloguing of whatever's behind it. CSG and the dragon government will pay for the time of the puzzle expert and lend us a dragon who can explain anything dragonish we might find inside. Hortplatz will house, feed, arrange transport back and forth, and provide physical labor and guides where necessary. In return for everybody's contributions, when the contents of the hoard have been catalogued, they will be divided equally according to their assigned value. Whatever's in there has been around for anywhere between nine and fifteen thousand years, so even if it's not diamonds, it's treasure." The historical value alone would be incredible—especially if the preservation spells kept the items from degrading.

"That sounds fair to me," Brandt begins, but I hold up a hand.

"I'm not finished, sorry. Once the contents have been divided and rehomed, this cave, the door, and all the puzzle pieces will become the property of the village of Hortplatz." I wanted a way to attract other species to the village… this is it. The number of community academics alone who'll come to stay and study the door and the hoard items the village keeps will be in the hundreds, if not thousands. If we make it a kind of museum and bring in the general public too…

"Alistair," David says, watching me, "you never told me your cousin was so intelligent."

Alistair beams. "Almost as smart as me!"

"Keep telling yourself that. All right, Garrett," he continues, "I'm not opposed to your suggestion. The lucifer will have to agree for CSG, of course, and I also want to add the stipulation that if we find anything of cultural significance to the dragons, it goes to them without being counted as part of their third."

I nod. "Of course. I'm not the British Museum."

A tiny smile teases his mouth. "And, if the village of Hortplatz presents its plans for the cave and they meet with CSG's approval, we would potentially be interested in providing sponsorship for any public facility that may eventuate and loaning our share of the items to that facility."

Yes! "That sounds good. Of course, I can't make any final agreements, but I'll present your offer to the village council." I really hope Damaris loves Asher enough to overlook how presumptuous I've been.

"This is delightful!" Brandt proclaims. "Now we just have to get it open."

We all turn to look at the massive metal-studded door. This is going to be so much fun.

CHAPTER THIRTY

Asher

AFTER A WHISPERED conversation with Micah and Zac, I teleport Garrett directly to Grandmother's house while they direct Caolan to open a portal back to our place.

"Asher?" she says when we find her in the living room. Her tone is cool, and I know she's still unhappy that we didn't tell her about the cave right away. "Is there a problem?"

"No. The opposite. Garrett's negotiated an amazing opportunity for us." I lay it on a little thick as I nudge him forward, but it *is* a great opportunity. Even if the contents of the vault are useless—or if it's empty—the door is an attraction itself. And Garrett fixed it so most of the work will be paid for by the government.

Garrett explains, his voice a bit shaky at first but growing in confidence when Grandmother doesn't immediately rip his throat out. She interrupts at one point to turn her gaze on me. "Call Jesse. The council needs to vote on this now, and then meet with the other parties. Or did they leave already?"

"They're waiting to meet with the council," I assure her. We made sure of that.

My call to Jesse is done when I feel the tingle of a teleport. It's Grandmother's house, so I don't call out to see who it is. She hates that.

"Grandmother?" a chorus of voices call, and her face softens slightly. Very slightly. Okay, if I hadn't been looking directly at her, I wouldn't have been able to tell the difference. But there *is* a difference, and it reminds me that she does love us all.

Chloe and Isaac burst into the room a second later, followed at a more sedate pace by Dad and Uncle Hal. "We've come for snacks," Dad declares, slapping me on the back. "Hello."

"I thought you might visit today," Uncle Hal says as I scoop up Chloe for a hug. She's so much bigger now, nearly eight, but I'm not willing to give this up just yet.

"We were planning to, but it was more complicated than we thought. I'll explain… just…" I turn to Grandmother. "Jesse said five minutes."

She inclines her head. "I'll go now, then. I want to fill him in first." She teleports out without another word.

"Does this mean no snacks?" Isaac asks. "Grandmother never goes when we visit."

"I'll get the snacks," Garrett tells him, grinning. "Come and help me find the cookie jar."

"Me too." Chloe squirms to be let down, then grabs his hand and tugs him toward the kitchen as Isaac races ahead. "I know where she hides the chocolate ones."

I wait until they've left the room, then fill Dad and Uncle Hal in on the events of the day. It's entertaining to see them react with such shock, it's written on their faces clear enough for any species to read.

"There's a dragon hoard within walking distance of here?" Uncle sputters.

"And the door is a giant puzzle?" Dad's eyes are wide.

"Did you say Garrett arranged for the town to own it?" Uncle adds.

I nod. "That's what Grandmother's doing right now, sorting it with the council. We'll get the puzzle expert out here to open the door, then catalogue whatever we find and set up a… I guess a museum of sorts. Garrett believes it will attract a lot of academics and tourists."

Dad smiles. "So even if we're slow to convince other species to move here, there will still be plenty of opportunities for us to mingle with them."

"Exactly. His main goal is still to get a more varied population of residents here, but he sees this as being an excellent stepping stone." Not to mention how good it is for the town. He's excited to be able to make this contribution.

"Looks like your marriage worked out well for us all," Uncle teases, and I chuckle. He has no idea. I still can't believe how much has happened today… that Garrett loves me and wants to stay married.

Dammit… does this mean I have to be grateful to Alistair for trying to set him up with someone else?

The kids return, cookies in hand, trailed by Garrett, who comes over and leans against me the way he always does. I love it. "I was just telling Chloe and Isaac that the cave has a secret room that a dragon put some things in, and someone is going to come and open it for us."

Isaac's eyes are big. "Are you really sure it wasn't Ed?"

"We're really sure," I tell him. "I don't know what this dragon's name was, but I can find out, if you like? She lived a long time ago, and she was only visiting here. It definitely wasn't Ed, and there's no dragon there now."

"But," Garrett adds, "there's going to be a dragon visiting when we get the door open. Maybe I can convince them to visit the school for some questions, *if* everyone promises not to go to the cave without an adult."

"Promise!" they both shout. "A real, live dragon?" Chloe adds, her voice breathy with excitement. Dad winces, and I know he's thinking that if we weren't so isolated, dragons would just have been part of her narrative by now. There might not be many of them, but they exist in the community.

"A real, live dragon," Garrett assures her. "And the person who's coming to open the cave makes special puzzles. Maybe he'll come and show you some."

Part of me wants to laugh that Garrett's already committing these experts to a Q&A at the school with the children, even though we don't know who they are and they haven't even committed to coming. But I know my husband… these strangers are going to talk to the kids and think it was their own idea.

I can't wait to see it happen.

ᛗ

It's WELL past dinnertime by the time Gideon and Alistair teleport into the house—our house, the one Garrett and I share with my cousins. We left Grandmother's when Micah called to tell us all the visitors had gone to meet with the council. Since then, we've been waiting on tenterhooks to see what the final decisions and plans are.

My cousin looks just as grumpy as always when he strides into the kitchen, Garrett's cousin practically bouncing behind him. "Is there food? I'm *starving*," Alistair declares. "I was ready to eat the table."

"We can do better than that," Zac says, opening the

fridge and pulling out some leftovers. "It needs five minutes, so you can tell us how it went while you wait."

"Are we expecting anyone else?" Micah asks. "Or did they leave already?"

"They've left," Gideon confirms as he slouches into a chair at the table. "We're only here because Alistair threatened me if we didn't come fill you all in."

"Threatened you with what?" I take a sip from the cup of tea Garrett made me. I never used to drink it much before, but since the wedding I've started having some when he does, and I have to say… it's nice. It'll never be coffee, but there's something about a hot, soothing drink with my husband.

"Karaoke." Gideon's tone makes it sound like the equivalent of execution, and I get it.

"You're saying it wrong," Alistair protests. "It's karaoke!"

"I love karaoke." Garrett gives me a pleading look. "Maybe next time we're in Zurich, we can find a karaoke bar?"

There aren't many things in the world that would be worse than that. "Sure," I reply, and Micah coughs to cover his laugh. He fails. I don't care, because Garrett's smiling.

"Okay, so… fill us in," Zac prompts.

"The council agreed with the plans that were discussed in the cave," Gideon begins. "They did add the proviso that someone nominated by the town council would be assigned to assist Alistair's friend—my take is that they're nervous about having someone they don't know play around with the puzzle they never knew existed, and want a babysitter they trust there."

"Fair enough," I concede. "If he's coming soon, we'd need someone to teleport him in and out of the cave anyway, and since there's no cell reception, they'd probably have to hang out there. Have they picked someone yet?"

"Micah," Gideon says, and Micah looks up from his phone.

"Yeah?"

"The council nominated you to babysit Al's puzzle friend." The slight twitch of Gideon's lips would be a full smirk on anyone else.

"What? But… why me?" The dismay in his voice is a joy to hear.

"Because you're an engineer and know more about shit like this than anyone else here."

Micah narrows his eyes at Gideon. "This was your idea."

"Yep. And I'm proud of it."

Before Micah can throw anything at Gideon's head, Garrett intervenes. "This is great—you'll get to watch each step of the puzzle. We're going to need someone who knows how it works when we open the museum."

Micah scowls but doesn't say anything, probably because he really does want to see how the puzzle works.

"Take good care of Cam," Alistair adds. "He's a bit absent sometimes. Gets lost in his puzzles and forgets things like food." He pauses. "It would help if you could wank a lot while he's here."

Glancing around the table, I can see I'm not the only one who doesn't know what to say. "Could… uh… what?"

"He's an incubus," Alistair explains. "And while I'm sure there's enough fucking here in the village to keep him fed, he's going to be spending most of his time *away* from the village, isn't he? Alone in that cave… except for Micah. So you need to make sure he's getting enough sex energy to stay healthy." He must see the shocked incomprehension on our faces. "Garrett, help me out here."

"I'll get some literature for them all," Garrett promises. "And I'll check in on Cam to make sure he's keeping well."

I know several incubi and succubae, but except for Garrett's colleague Annie, they all live in Zurich, and I never had to think about how they fed. Sexual energy, sure… and I know that doesn't have to mean actual sex… but what *does* it mean?

"Do we have an arrival date for him yet?" Garrett adds, and Alistair nods as the microwave timer goes off.

"Two weeks. He's finishing up some projects and putting his affairs in order, and then he'll be ready. He says from the looks of the pictures we sent, it could take anywhere from a week to a month to get done, depending on what happens as he goes along."

Micah doesn't look thrilled by that, and I'm enormously cheerful at the thought of my cousin having to sit in a cold cave all day, being ignored by an "absent" incubus.

Zac brings loaded plates to the table, and Alistair and Gideon dig in.

"So we've got two weeks to prepare for Cam," Garrett says. "Did Brandt say anything about the dragon we'll need when the door is open?"

Alistair swallows a mouthful. "He said to leave it with him and keep him informed of progress. I think he has someone in mind."

"We'll set up a shared server for this project," Gideon adds. "All progress reports and other information can be uploaded there. Garrett, the town council has nominated you to be Hortplatz's representative."

Garret's jaw drops. "Me?" he squeaks. "But I'm not even a demon."

This time, Gideon's smirk is plain as day. "But, as Grandmother said, you *are* a resident of this town, you're qualified for the job, and it was all your idea. You're family now, Garrett. There's no escaping us."

I lean over to kiss my husband's cheek. "Good thing Cambridge isn't expecting you back until July."

Garrett looks around the table, then leans against me. "I think I'm done with Cambridge. It's been fun, but they'll notice soon that I'm not aging like a human… and anyway, what do I need a university for when there's so much to keep me here?" He grins. "I think I'm going to stick with my demons-in-law."

༄

Thanks for reading *Asher*! Micah's book is next, as he and puzzle expert Cam work on getting the door open.

If you're new to this world, I recommend checking out *Demons Do It Better*, aka where Sam met Gideon and it all began.

We talk spoilers in my Facebook reader group, RoMMance with Becca & Louisa.
Or you can subscribe to my newsletter to get all updates and access to bonus scenes: https://bit.ly/LouisaMBonus.

For early access to chapters of my upcoming books, artwork, and other bonus material, check out my Patreon here: patreon.com/louisamasters

ALSO BY LOUISA MASTERS

Saddles & Suits

Alistair's Extraordinaries

Grave Situation

Elemental Men: The Complete Series

Style Me

Rebrand

Couture

Elf Magic

Wooing the Wiccan

Enticing the Elf

The Collective

Higher Demon

Demon Hunter

Demons-In-Law

Asher

Micah

Zachary

Franklin U

Mr. Romance

The Holigay Hookup *related novella

Batting Style

Ghostly Guardians

Spirited Situation

Vortex Conundrum

Conduit Crisis

Gateway Catastrophe

Here Be Dragons

Dragon Ever After

The Professor's Dragon

The Dragon Experiment

Conspiracy of Dragons

Hidden Species

Demons Do It Better

One Bite With A Vampire

Hijinks With A Hellhound

Sorcerers Always Satisfy

Hidden Species Box Set

Met His Match

Charming Him

Offside Rules

A Christmas Chance (novella)

Between the Covers (M/F)

Joy Universe

I've Got This

Follow My Lead

In Your Hands

Take Us There

Louisa Masters started reading romance much earlier than her mother thought she should. As an adult, she feeds her addiction in every spare second. She spent years trying to build a "sensible" career, working in bookstores, recruitment, resource management, administration, and as a travel agent before finally conceding defeat and devoting herself to the world of romance novels.

Louisa has a long list of places first discovered in books that she wants to visit, and every so often she overcomes her loathing of jet lag and takes a trip that charges her imagination. She lives in Melbourne, Australia, where she whines about the weather for most of the year while secretly admitting she'll probably never move.

http://www.louisamasters.com